THE DRACULA JOURNALS

Book 3

ETERNAL MIDNIGHT

Books by Thom Reese

The Infusion of Archie Lambert
The Empty
A Savage Distance
The Demon Baqash
Chasing Kelvin
Dead Man's Fire
13 Bodies
The Crimson Soul of Nathan Greene

The Dracula Journals *series*
The Dracula Journals: Dark Decades
The Dracula Journals: Ravaged Souls
The Dracula Journals: Eternal Midnight

THE DRACULA JOURNALS

Book 3

ETERNAL MIDNIGHT

Thom Reese

SPEAKING VOLUMES, LLC
NAPLES, FLORIDA
2019

THE DRACULA JOURNALS: ETERNAL MIDNIGHT

ISBN 978-1-64540-107-0

To my faithful readers.
You know who you are.

ACKNOWLEDGMENTS

Writing the Dracula Journals series has been a thrill, a challenge, a joy, a frustration, a delight, and pretty much any other emotion a person can have while riding the creative road. There has been fulfillment and apprehension. Throughout the process I've felt the shadow of Bram Stoker washing across my pages. It's a daunting prospect to write a series featuring one of the best known and loved characters of all time. I hope I've done it justice. But the truth is, I couldn't have done it without people to support and encourage me. So, thank you so much to all of you who have come along beside me to help this novel come to be. As always, my wonderful wife Kathy has been there to keep me on course. My daughters, Trista, Amy, and Brittany inspire my every breath even though they are now physically distant. Thank you, Jeff Granstrom and Crystal Hill for your comments and suggestions on my early drafts. Your input is invaluable. As always, thank you to Kurt and Erica Mueller at Speaking Volumes for their faith in me as a writer. And thank you to my loyal readers who make this endeavor worthwhile. You are all very much appreciated!

The following is a collection of letters, journal entries, newspaper clippings, and other writings found in the home of Peter Van Helsing *in August 2015. They have been organized in such a way as to allow the reader to best follow the sequence of events as they transpired. All entries unrelated to the topic at hand have been eliminated in order that these testimonies may stand on their own merit without distraction or confusion.*

From the journal of Vlad Dracula
June 17, 1986

She was in a small three room home. The rotted remains of what I assume to be a father and young daughter sat at the dining room table, their flesh gray and taut, their eyes gazing sightlessly into eternity. The remains of numerous beasts littered the floor: two large dogs, several rats, a feline, a crow. Each had been savaged for blood. Lavinia sat at a small Casio keyboard playing a haunting melody.

She had been the first to receive my blood as a passage into the eternal midnight of the nosferatu—the vampire. I performed the crimson miracle on her some four centuries past. She had been my bride, the first among many in this dark existence, and for a time, she stood at the center of my every thought. Lavinia had been feisty, with a wicked grin and a lethal humor. Her hair was long and dark, her form curvaceous, her appetite for blood ravenous. Our times together had been as beautiful as they were garish. Our desires had known no bounds.

"Lavinia," I said. "At last I have found you."

She continued to play, ignoring me. Her eyes were wide, her expression vacant. A swatch of flesh had been ripped from her right cheek. A flap of skin hung limply just above her chin, a clear evidence of her weakened state, for such a wound should heal with little difficulty.

"Lavinia," I repeated. "I am here."

She began the song anew, increasing the volume.

I stepped forward, slapping the keyboard from its stand. It skittered across the floor and settled upside down, a scrap of plastic shooting off to the left. A single wavering note continued to sound. Lavinia stared forward, not toward me, but to where the keyboard now lay. Her eyes were glassy and unfocused. "I have come for you," said I.

She laughed, low and throaty. Drool slipped over her bottom lip. "The master returns. Oh! I must celebrate." Here, she leaped to her feet to begin dancing about the small room in quick graceless bounds. Her matted and bloodstained hair whipped about, her bare feet stuttered and hopped. Her sheer cotton dress was shredded and bloodstained. One breast was exposed as was a buttock. "Vlad has returned," she shouted. "Oh, how happy I suppose you think I should be." She then arced her head back and spat, sending spittle directly above her to then fall onto her left cheek with a splat. She gave no visible sign that she even noticed the substance on her face, but began singing the song she had played on the electronic keyboard. "There is a house in New Orleans." She screamed the words, venom in her voice. "That puppy's called the rising sun."

I was appalled. I had crossed an ocean to recover my lost bride. Lavinia had, in recent months, become an obsession. Though, admittedly, I had thought little of her for decades, suddenly she dominated my every thought, my every desire. Had I traveled all this way back to Europe, searched for all of these months, only to find a mad woman?

"Where are your two companions?" I asked, remaining calm, ignoring her nonsense. Obviously her mental state had deteriorated. "Do they yet live?" I referred to two lesser brides I had left in her service when I relocated to London more than a hundred years past.

One hundred years!

Truly, this thought struck me dumb. Had it been so long ago? Why then would I even concern myself with Lavinia? What twisted specter in my soul had dredged her up to become my insatiable desire?

She giggled, shaking her head, causing her hair to spill over her face in dark matted clumps. "Your two whores? My replacements! Vlad's little replacement brides."

"Yes. The other brides. Do they live?" I had left Lavinia in charge, the other two were to act as her helpmates. In truth I cared little for them—even their names escape me—but I was curious about Lavinia's existence over these long decades. Had she taken any comfort in the companionship of those of her own kind?

"Do they live? Do they live!" She repeated this over and over, her voice rising in volume till she was screaming near incomprehensibly.

"Yes!" I bellowed. "Do they live? It is a simple question."

Lavinia spun, twirling on the tips of her toes as would a ballerina. "And why does the great Vlad Dracula care? Are each of his brides not disposable? It would seem we are."

"I have come back for you. That should be answer enough. As to the others, they were never your equals, but still I ask, do they live?"

Lavinia chuckled, licking her lips as she did so. She stepped toward me. "No. They do not live—*master*!" The last word was issued with spite and venom. "Our state was precarious, our food scarce. And so I chose to survive."

"Obviously you survived. What became of them?"

"I was older in the eternal midnight than them. Stronger physically and mentally. And so I bound them each like cattle to a hitch and drank from them. Each night, long and sweet until there was nothing left to consume." She grinned. "Their blood was sweet. It tasted. Something. Like. You!"

And then she bound on me, clamping her fangs on my neck.

My first instinct was to throw her from me, to twist her ungrateful head from her shoulders, to toss her corpse to the street. But I allowed her to feed. Her odor was horrid, her formerly beautiful face contorted and gaunt. She drew from me in loud reckless gulps, slurping and gurgling. It was revolting, but my blood was strong and she had obviously fared poorly. I could endure the insult for there was once a time when she had been precious to me. Perhaps an infusion of my robust blood might even help to restore her sanity.

She drank for nearly ten minutes before I pulled her away. Here, she growled and grappled attempting to continue feeding. "No!" I yelled and slapped her, an act which caused her to stumble backward, landing on her backside. I stepped forward. "Enough," I said. "I have come for you and I reclaim you as mine. Now, rise. It is time you leave this dismal existence to resume your former station."

I turned and strolled from the hovel convinced that I no longer cared if she accompanied me. But the truth of it is, my heart gave a bit of a leap when, perhaps two minutes later, Lavinia followed.

From the journal of Vlad Dracula
December 9, 1989

I would never claim to be a patient man. One might conclude that since I count my existence not in mere decades but in centuries that I might have acquired the trait. And perhaps, to an extent, I have. But it has never been my nature. But these years since my return, the years of rehabilitating Lavinia have perhaps granted me some small trace of forbearance.

For months, she fed from my veins alone, my robust blood renewing her physically. The scars that had marred her face and body gradually faded to nothing. Her form, which had become angular and nearly misshapen, filled out, her luxurious curves returned, her breasts once again became ripe and inviting.

But her mind.

Oh, but that her mind had healed so quickly. For she was broken from within. Rebellious and disdainful. And beastlike. I would frequently discover her crawling about on all fours, sniffing at the floor, licking the walls, or perhaps howling at the night birds. At times I would shout at her. "What do you do, woman? Have you no sense remaining?"

Frequently such a retort would be followed by a throaty chuckle from Lavinia or a dismissive string of profanities. Or worse, a strangled chorus from one of those horrid rock and roll songs for which she had acquired a taste. Many times I considered simply ending her. I could have easily opened her veins and bled her into oblivion. In truth, I do not know what prevented me from following this thought to its conclusion.

But Lavinia has always held the capacity to stimulate. And perhaps I have allowed her too much freedom where this is concerned. She has never been my equal and certainly never will attain such a status, but there is a certain fire within the girl that enchants me. One could argue that I am a slave to her beauty, but I believe it goes deeper than that. For the world is populated with beautiful maidens and I have sampled many. But, despite myself, I return to Lavinia. Peculiar. I do wonder what a mere barmaid could possess to stir me so.

Eventually, though, I did tire of her unpredictable ways for I desired a companion not an inmate. And so I sought to give her access to the one truly curative substance a nosferatu may consume. Blood. Yes, of course it was blood. But not any blood, but the blood of the innocent. I cannot explain why there is a difference or what that particular distinction might be. But I can state most assuredly that taking blood from an innocent is much more revitalizing than that taken from a scoundrel.

And so I took Lavinia to an orphanage.

The place was operated by nuns and therefore rife with hideous crucifixes. But this was a problem easily remedied. For the cross itself holds little power over me. It is the person baring the cross that grants the symbol sway. And that person must possess a level of belief in order to activate the damning properties within. Certainly some number of these sisters would possess such commitment—but not all. Perhaps not even most. To this point, I was able to lure a young sister to me while she gathered supplies at a nearby market one eve. She smiled at me nervously, a slight quiver to her lips, but the flush of excitement on her cheeks. I sensed in her a conflict, a level of regret for giving up perpetually the joys of physical passion, but then a grief for having this same desire, which she perceived as a weakness. Whatever would her Lord think of her?

She was attracted to me, both sexually and for the sheer thrill of adventurous disobedience. I angled my head, leading her from the market and into an adjacent alleyway. She nearly turned away, fright and guilt attempting to quell her excitement. But her blood was rife with desire and her faith, while real, was not quite so strong as her suddenly surging hormones.

She came to me.

I granted her my blood.

And oh did she moan with pleasure and release. Few have ever given themselves so willing or completely as did this young naïve nun. For once the decision to break her vow was made she embraced what she saw as perhaps the one deviation she would ever allow with gusto.

And she became my willing thrall.

When our pleasure was complete, I then instructed her to clear the dormitory of crosses and to admit us entrance and privacy on the designated eve. I felt no resistance as she smiled, cooing at me and gazing into my eyes.

And on the designated night, Lavinia's feast was to be incomparable.

It was a near moonless eve. The well-worn hallways were silent for the nuns had retired soon after the children. My pet nun led us to a doorway at the end of the corridor and then told us that the children were within. As a reward for her efforts I bit my lower lip and then allowed her to suck blood from the tiny wound. Grinning, she told me that she was mine eternally. I assume she had made a similar vow to her God.

There were four young females within, each appearing to be between eight and ten years of age. They were asleep upon our arrival. They did not remain so for long.

Lavinia was as a rabid dog. There was no finesse, no attempt to calm her victims or to make the deaths painless. She ripped into the first child before the girl had regained consciousness. Nearly inhaling the blood, she gulped and guzzled noisily waking the other children. Of course their instinct was to scream, but I pushed my way into their simple child minds, quieting them and holding them docile for my mate.

Once finished with the first child, she tossed the limp form onto the girl's narrow cot and moved to the next, ravaging her throat as she had the previous child. I could sense the remaining children struggling against my hold as they watched the splay of blood spat across Lavinia's face. These were not thralls, for they had not received my blood. As such, my hold was tentative. Some minds, I may control quite easily absent the blood connection, others not at all. These were children and therefore more susceptible. Still, they pushed, wishing desperately to flee.

Oh and how Lavinia laughed at this devilish drama, wiping the crimson liquid from her cheeks with a palm and then licking her hand clean before returning to the main course. It was such a delight to watch her work. For the first time since our reunion, I felt true longing for my companion.

By the time she approached the fourth child I could sense a difference in her. The movements were smooth, nearly feline. No longer did she lumber and lope. Even her attack had attained subtleties. Though she was bathed in gore, she smiled sweetly at the final girl, whispering to her, comforting her as she flinched. When finally teeth penetrated flesh the process was so delicate as to be nearly unnoticeable.

After, when each child lay lifeless about the room, she came to me, a luscious grin skirting her lips. "Vlad," she said. "It has been long and longer. I am correct, am I not?"

I nodded, cupping her chin in my hand. "It has, my dear."

"Then, may I suggest we wait no longer?" And before I could respond, she dropped her garment and allowed me to take her there amidst the lifeless children.

Transcript of a Video Recording Made by Peter Van Helsing
March 23, 2014

PETER: Okay. Right. Here we are. Alright, as you can see behind me, I'm at the airport, O'Hare International—heading out to Romania! So, here's the deal. For those of you new to my vids, I'm Peter Van Helsing. Van Helsing! Like the vampire hunter in Bram Stoker's Dracula novel. The thing is, until a few months ago I thought my last name was Kubler. That's my mom's maiden name. So if you've been following my vids on YouTube you probably know me by that name. See, my dad died when I was four and Mom kept me away from his family, didn't want me to know anything about the Van Helsings.

Wanna guess why?

Yeaaah. Vampires.

Here's the kicker. They're real. No. Seriously. My great, great uncle—or maybe great, great, great, I'm not really sure. Anyway, he was Abraham Van Helsing, one of the guys responsible for Dracula's death back in the 1890s.

Yeah, that's right. Dracula is real.

And he's alive again. Actually, he has been since the 1930s.

That's radical. Just nuts. You probably don't believe me, but just hang in there. This thing's going to be wild.

So, here's the deal. Once I found out my true heritage, I started digging. Ends up my family has been fighting vampires, and Dracula in particular, for decades. And it was Dracula that killed my dad. That's when my mom took me away from the Van Helsings. I get it, but God! Dracula!

Yeah. So I was late to the party. But I'm an industrious guy. Once I get a whiff of something I just can't let it go. Guess that's why I became a reporter. And when I got news of our family history from my mom's brother Don, well, boom! There I went. After the truth, I mean. I had to learn everything I could.

You see, my Dad's sister, Lizzy, and her husband, Conner, had a whole trunk full of stuff that originated with Abraham Van Helsing. It had made its way across the Atlantic to my great Uncle Charlie—and eventually into their hands.

Okay, so here's a quick Van Helsing family tree history lesson. After my dad died back in the seventies, after my Aunt Lizzy's failed attempt to kill Dracula, after she and Conner spent another decade clearing Chicago of vampires—did I mention that Dracula was in Chicago? Well, they never caught another whiff of Dracula. So they hid the trunk away at one of those self-storage places. I'm guessing they didn't want Dracula to track down those documents—the original journal pages collected to create Bram Stoker's novel, the translations of Dracula's original journal, all of the case files detailing the vampire hunts, and Conner's record of his own experience on an island populated by vampires. That's its own crazy story. So we'll save that for another video. Maybe he'll let me interview him.

Anyway. So, obviously I've read them. All of the journals, the case files, everything. Crazy stuff. Chilling. But, cool. You see, I'm an investigative reporter. I do documentaries—just like this one. I dig things up that weren't meant to be found. The Van Helsings own a private detective agency—and weirdly enough, a bunch of laundromats. Looking through Van Helsing Investigations financials, I found a yearly outlay for a storage unit beginning in 1988, just about the time Lizzy and Conner stopped actively hunting monsters. As you might expect, I was curious. Curiosity is my thing. And I have that Pitbull gene. I won't let something go once I get the scent.

Ever.

Drives people nuts. But, hey, if you're not all-in, why bother at all, right?

So, here's the he-didn't-just-say-that part. I think I've found Dracula. Not physically. Not yet at least. I'm still at the airport, right? Still en route. But on paper. I've got his address. No bull. This is real.

You see, my Aunt Lizzy, Uncle Conner, and their colleagues cleared Chicago of vampires back in the eighties. No new activity in decades. To me, that meant that Dracula was no longer there. Right? I mean, if he was here, he'd be busy making a new fang gang to keep him company or whatever. So, if he wasn't in Chicago, where was he?

Exactly.

So I went searching, looking for reports of vampiric activity. None. Not here in the States at least. So I started thinking, where would he go? Well, back home, right? Wouldn't that make sense? Things got too tough here. Maybe the Van Helsings were getting too close for comfort, maybe he just needed to chill, maybe he just needed to rest in home soil. His reason doesn't matter. The thing is, I started searching for evidence of him in Romania. His home turf.

And you know what? Yeaaaah. He's there.

He bought a castle back in the early nineties. Oh, not under his own name, but he bought it. Rural area. Very isolated. And there've been stories. Strange tales of bloodless corpses and abnormal animal behavior ever since the castle was bought. Oh, of course everyone thinks these are just stories from backward-thinking uneducated people, but we know better, don't we?

So, here's the part that psyches me. I'm going after him. Yeah, I know. Insane, right? I'm going after Dracula—the real Dracula! Never thought I'd be saying that.

I'm going to video the whole thing, make a whole documentary. I want to see if he can be caught on video. I want to prove to the world that vampires are real.

Now, I know what you're thinking. What's this guy know about hunting vampires? Well, I'm a Van Helsing. I got family vampire hunting blood on my side. And I've read all of the vampire-related records and journal entries from my ancestors—the real experts. I got a pretty good handle on this thing. Besides, I'm not really trying to take Dracula down. No, my gig is to expose him. After that, he'll be on the run. I mean, if I can document an encounter with Dracula or maybe other vampires, if I can record it and get it out to the world, well, then people who know what they're doing—the military, cops, Ghostbusters, whatever—could come in and clear them out for good. Half of Dracula's power is that nobody really believes in him, right? I'm not saying that I can kill him and I'm not saying that I can't. If I get the chance, sure, I'll take a stab at it. Yeah. Pun intended. But my real goal is to get the word out, get some video of him and his kind. Dracula's only safe as long as the world doesn't believe in him. Well, I'm going to make sure they know.

So, that's the deal. It's about time to board my plane. Stay tuned on my YouTube channel for updates. It's going to be a wild ride. That's a promise.

From the Files of Van Helsing Investigations
April 4, 2014

CASE NUMBER 407

NOTES FROM APRIL 4, 2014
AS RECORDED BY LIZZY VAN HELSING-MULLIGAN
RE: INITIAL DISCUSSION & STRATEGY
CONCERNING PETER VAN HELSING

I haven't seen my nephew Peter since he was a young boy. He'd be what, 42 now? Something like that. The last time I saw him he was four. The man on the video was a stranger. He could have been anyone. But it was Peter. I didn't recognize the man, but I did see family characteristics. That mix of Haitian and Caucasian that I and my brothers shared—our mother was Haitian our father Caucasian. Peter's mother is Caucasian, making him one quarter Haitian. His skin is dark, but not black. Caramel might be a good description. Peter's features are clearly Haitian. He has the hint of my brother's so-sarcastic grin. I see the shape of my mother's eyes when he grins. He looks to be taller than his dad and has bleached his hair to blond. It's long and pulled back into a pony tail. On the video, he was wearing a tank top, a head band, and a nose ring in his left nostril. He wore a backpack with bongos tied to the side and a speaker blaring The Dave Matthews Band hanging from his belt.

He in no way seems the type that should be tracking vampires. I contacted his wife, Vanessa. She informed me that they're divorced and hung up on me. I've since learned that he cashed in his retirement accounts four months ago and quit his job the day before he intended to leave for Europe.

He has two children. What could he be thinking?

It's been decades since Conner and I have hunted vampires—we're in our seventies after all. But Peter is family. And past our prime or not we can't let him run off and hunt Dracula alone. My brothers and I literally grew up fighting these monsters and both brothers and both of my parents died as a result. What hope could Peter have? And so we called a family meeting to discuss our options. To figure out just how in the hell we could get to Peter before it was too late.

In addition to Conner and myself, our son Dane was in attendance along with Peter's mother Sheri. An associate of ours from Van Helsing Investigations, Kerri Rivera, was also present, though Connor and I are now only marginally involved with the firm.

Dane's in his thirties, Kerri, her forties. They both volunteered to fly to Romania to intercept Peter, stating that Conner and I are much too old for such adventuring. And we are too old, but that doesn't mean we shouldn't go. And even if Dane and Kerri accompany us, I have very little confidence in our success. Kerri works as an investigator, but was never involved in the hunt. She is fully capable of sitting in a car taking pictures of unfaithful husbands or for searching through piles of files looking for evidence of doctored books. But as much as she'd like to think of herself as some sort of female James Bond, she's more of a socially awkward desk jockey.

As to Dane…

He's my son. I love him. But, he's never had any interest in this area of our lives. He opted out of involvement in either of the family businesses. He's drifted through several lucrative and influential positions but never seems content to settle.

But I'm getting ahead of myself. Peter's video left us very little information. A country. He said what country he would be in. No region, no city. He didn't reveal what name Dracula was going by. We could assume Dracula would head to the region of Wallachia—his home territory, but even that's a guess. Wallachia was Dracula's mortal homeland but as a vampire he'd purchased land in Transylvania. Perhaps that would hold more of a draw.

Sheri was a wreck, screaming at Conner and me. "It's all your fault. You damn Van Helsings." She hollered this over and over until her voice began to sound hoarse.

Once she'd worn down some I said, "Sheri, we've stayed out of Peter's life for nearly forty years specifically so that this would never happen. We never wanted him dragged into this. We haven't pursued vampires ourselves in something like twenty-five years."

"But he found your records. You left them where he could find them. You lured him into taking over for you because you're too old to do it yourselves."

Her argument was ridiculous. We all knew it. She probably even knew it at some level. She was a frightened mother and needed someone to blame for putting her son at risk. The fact that Peter had illegally acquired these documents through breaking and entering was of no concern to her. In her eyes we'd been responsible for her husband's death and now we'd be responsible for her son's as well. The worst of it was that I *was* responsible for Stephen's death. I'd been the one to pull him back in. I'd been anxious, I'd wanted my older brother.

"Listen," said Conner. "You're the one who sent us the link to Peter's video. Obviously, you wanted our help. We called this meeting because we're concerned for Peter. You may not like the Van Helsing side of Peter's family, so be it. But you can either help us come up with a plan to find your son and get him home safely or you can waste our time with accusations. If that's all you have to offer, I suggest you leave."

Conner's not much for small talk. Even less for nonsense. It's his military background, I guess. Or maybe the trauma and loss he's experienced. He'd spent about a decade in a drug induced haze after surviving several months on an island inhabited primarily by vampires. But once he'd come back to his right mind he became an efficient focused individual with little tolerance for erratic behavior.

"He's my son," said Sheri.

"And we're here to figure out a way to get him home safely. So either become an asset or show yourself to the door."

Sheri's about my age, but much more frail. She shows her advanced years. Her bone-like hands often shake, her hair is thin and wispy, she walks with a cane, there's a tick to her left eye. It seemed as though Conner's words hit her with the force of a physical assault. She started to cry, burying her face in her twittering hands. I said, "Sheri, I know you don't like us. You blamed us for Stephen's death and I can't say that you were wrong. Stevie was my brother and I've carried that guilt for decades. But, at your insistence, we've had nothing to do with Peter. Our only purpose here is to bring him home safely—even at risk to our own lives. So, please. You're the only one here who knows Peter. Help us to know what he might do, how he might act in extreme situations."

She glared at Conner for several seconds before nodding. Wiping a tear from her cheek with a crooked knuckle she said, "Peter. What might he do?" Here, she chuckled. "Well, he's impulsive. That much, I'm sure you've already guessed. He doesn't really think things through. Oh, he's very intelligent with big impressive ideas, but not very good at dealing with reality. He's one of those free spirits."

"Why would he go after Dracula?" This from my son Dane who leaned against the wall to Sheri's right, arms crossed, an expression that could be interpreted as disinterest on his face.

"Peter… He always liked the idea of grand adventures or accomplishments. He envisions himself as something greater than what his life would suggest."

Conner said, "He said he was an investigative reporter."

Sheri chuckled. "Oh, that. He's referring to his YouTube documentaries. He's convinced he'll be the next big rave. His real job was working at Best Buy for the Geek Squad. Like I said, Peter likes to think of himself as some sort of high achiever."

Dane said, "Interesting insight coming from a mother. I'd have thought you'd want to build up our opinion of Peter." And then he paused, smiled. "But maybe not. You want us to be concerned. You want us to realize how foolhardy your son can be. Hey, my boy's a doofus. Please race across the ocean and risk your own neck to save him from his own stupidity. That about right?"

Sheri stared at him, apparently uncertain how to respond. "Peter and I… We don't often see eye-to-eye. Especially since his divorce. It was his fault… Mostly. We're, I suppose you could call it estranged."

I said, "None of this explains why he'd be so reckless. He had a wife, he has children."

She offered a tight grin. "Peter's ex-wife took the children, hired a good attorney, and moved the children out of state. Though he's reckless and irresponsible, those children were the light in his life. He probably thought his bravery would impress the kids, maybe even get his family back. He thinks his grand adventures impress people. Maybe they will impress his children, I don't know. But his wife couldn't take any more of it. He was just too unpredictable. The judge in their divorce agreed with her; she received full custody."

Conner and I made eye contact. The image portrayed was not of the kind of man that could hope to survive an encounter with a vampire—particularly Dracula.

"Sheri," said Conner. "We need access to Peter's home. We need to get onto his computer, look through his files, see if he left anything behind that could get us started. And we need to do it now."

Even as Conner said this, I feared it might already be too late. Peter was already in Europe. For all we knew he already had a line on Dracula's locale.

Transcript of a Video Recording Made by Peter Van Helsing
April 05, 2014

PETER: Greetings from Romania. Wow. I am actually in Romania! How cool is that? My first international broadcast!

Now, if you remember from my previous segment, I'm hear tracking the legendary vampire Dracula. See the previous vid for details.

So, I know you've heard of Transylvania—and, in case you're out of the loop, that's in present day Romania. But while Dracula did eventually buy property in Transylvania, his true home was Wallachia—also in present day Romania. And that's where I'm heading. That's where he's hiding.

Look at this place!

I don't know how much you know about the country—you probably have images of the old black and white Universal horror films like Dracula and Frankenstein. But, Romania has a special vibe all its own. I guess I should probably tell you a little bit about it, give you the backdrop, the landscape, all the nitty gritty, before we hit the trail in search of Dracula!

So, I flew into Bucharest, which, fortunately, isn't that far from Wallachia. Big plus there. The place has this old classic vibe to it. Not that it hasn't moved into the twenty-first century—it has. Oh, yeah. There are cars, cell phones, the internet, TV, the media and everything you would expect. But the look of the place. Wow. Just absolutely not the U.S. of A. Traditional. Yeah. I guess that would be the word. The architecture feels like its centuries old. I mean, I'm no expert. I couldn't even name one architectural style. Well, Tudor, I've heard of Tudor. But I wouldn't know one if I smacked into it. And Victorian. I could probably pick that out. But, hey, that has nothing to do with this. Let's just say this: Romania—old looking.

Wow. That description sucks. Sorry. I should've done more cultural research or something.

Anyway, so here we go with some details. The business people wear modern western looking clothing, but I see a lot of what I would call traditional regional clothing intermingled. Very colorful, very… traditional. From what I'm told, this type of garb will become more prominent as I make my way to the rural areas.

And the people, they're, I guess formal would be the term. Very friendly, but formal. I don't speak Romanian. I learned a few words in preparation for the trip, but yeah, not enough. But, in the city at least, I've come across enough English speakers to help me along. So, formal, yeah. Don't address anyone by their first name. At least not right away. Mister or Missus, that kind of thing. That's what they're looking for. And always shake hands. I see some people doing that two cheek kiss thing. No one's done that to me yet. I think I stand out pretty obviously as a tourist.

That's probably okay, right? I mean, they'll know I need a little guidance and may not know their traditions—which apparently are a big deal here.

So, okay. Here's the plan. I'm staying at an inn tonight and then renting a car to drive to Wallachia tomorrow. But I'll be heading into the rural area where I believe Dracula to be. Apparently, the area's pretty backwards. I guess I'll just need to kind of, you know, wing it from there.

We'll see what happens, huh?

Alright. That's it for this time. See you in a few.

Transcript of a Video Recording Made by Peter Van Helsing April 07, 2014

PETER: Hello again. Peter Van Helsing here with part three of my Romanian adventure series—In Search of Dracula!

So, the last couple of days, wow, pretty stressful. Beautiful country. Stunning. Gorgeous mountains, crystal blue rivers. At the risk of sounding cliché, breathtaking. But I got lost three separate times. The maps around here, I don't want to say they suck, but God I wish I could catch Google Maps right now. But cell reception's spotty out here. Pretty much hit and miss.

I'm headed pretty far off any well-traveled roads, so it's a challenge. I've received several emails from my Aunt Lizzy—the vampire hunter! Okay, got some from my mom too. Hi, Mom. I'm fine. Stop freaking. Lizzy and Conner, you can stop worrying too. I get it. You don't think I can do this. Well, you don't know me. And you don't know what I'm capable of. I'm as much a Van Helsing as you are, Lizzy. Some of that had to get passed down to me, right?

Wow. Sorry for the family sidebar. Back to business.

I've read every one of Dracula's journal entries and all of the vampire related documents my Uncle Conner hid away. I've got crucifixes and garlic oil. I'm going to buy some knives here and etch crosses into them. I've read about all of the Van Helsing vampire hunting techniques. I'm stoked and ready to go.

Again, my goal is not to kill Dracula and the other vampires, but to expose them. The vampire hunting gear is primarily for protection. And we'll just see how things roll from there. You never know what'll happen.

That's why it's an adventure, right?

Okay. So, here's the update.

I've made my way to a village that's maybe thirty miles from Dracula's suspected locale. Thirty miles. Not that far, but out here, not so close. No roads lead to the castle. They were all washed out in a flood a couple of decades back and never repaired.

Shortly after the man I suspect to be Dracula purchased the castle.

Coincidence? Nah. Let's be real.

So, no passable roads leading to the castle. I guess I shouldn't think it would be easy. No problem. I'm in good shape. As you know from previous vids, I've done some major rock climbing and repelling. No big issues here. I'll proceed on foot.

I've been asking around about the castle, about the man who owns it, about any weird, freako happenings.

No one wants to talk.

No one.

I mean, this is the twenty-first century, right? But any talk that sounds like its heading toward the topic of vampires and people cross themselves and mutter in Romanian and just walk away. Just walk away!

So, I guess you could call them superstitious. But then, is it really superstitious if the thing they fear actually exists? I mean, if I'm correct and Dracula is less than fifty miles away, they've probably seen vampiric activity down here in these villages, right? Dracula's got to feed. So maybe it's not so much superstitious as firsthand knowledge.

Maybe some of these people have even seen him!

So, that's my next goal. Find some people and talk with them. Maybe get some down and dirty lowdown on Dracula.

See you next time. Later.

Transcript of a Video Recording Made by Peter Van Helsing
April 08, 2014

PETER: Hey, all. Peter Van Helsing here with part four of my Romanian adventure—In Search of Dracula!

So, I met a girl. No, no. Not like that. We're not hooking up or anything.

Anyway, here's the deal. After some persuasion involving the offer of two hundred dollars American, she's offered to act as my guide. Her name's Anica. She's a twenty-something year-old village girl who's just returned from Cambridge University. She's back visiting her parents before starting a government job in Bucharest. Speechwriter for some politician. Her English is excellent, which is how we ended up talking. Her pronunciations are British, but she has an underlying Romanian accent. I guess exotic would describe her speech. Kind of sexy—if I was looking. Which I'm not!

We hit it off pretty well. Laughing and joking. I guess she's what my mom always says about me—a free spirt. Especially for someone with her traditional upbringing.

So, what else? Her language training was formal and so her speech—at least in English—is very proper sounding. She seems much freer when interacting with her fellow villagers in her native tongue. With me, very proper pronunciations even though her attitude is fun and energetic.

When I told her that I needed a guide to Ungur Castle—that's where I suspect Dracula to be—she said her parents are very superstitious and would be "terribly afraid" if they knew where we were going. So she's telling them that I've hired her to show me the countryside. I don't think they like the idea. It's not appropriate in their eyes. I'm a foreign male—practically twice Anica's age and not at all traditional—traipsing off alone with their little girl. But hey, let's put this on the table right now. There's nothing inappropriate happening. At least, not inappropriate in the way her parents might be thinking. Again, not hooking up!

So, here's the plan. If all goes well, Anica will get me close to the castle and then turn around and head back here. I don't want to be responsible for her encountering Dracula. That wouldn't be cool.

So, yeah. Segue to my preparations. I bought some totally rad daggers. They're very sharp. And narrow. Seven or eight inches in length. A dozen of them, as many as the local general store had. The shopkeeper looked at me like I was some kind of Charles Manson. Which will probably make Anica's parents freak even worse. It's a small village. We all know word will get to them, right?

So, I prepped the daggers, etched crosses into them, bathed them in garlic oil. That stuff stinks, by the way. So, I've got my vampire-fighting arsenal: daggers, crosses, garlic. I've got a guide, a backpack with a four day supply of nuts and bread. There was no freeze-dried food available like I'd find at a camping supply store in the U.S. We leave in the morning. I'm stoked.

Tune in for the next segment. We'll be on the trail—In Search of Dracula!

Later.

Transcript of a Video Recording Made by Peter Van Helsing
April 09, 2014

PETER: Hey. Peter Van Helsing here. What is this, segment five?

So, this is weird. I don't know how else to say it. Just weird. Bizarre. We're being followed by a pack of wolves. Yeah. Freaky. They've been with us for about three hours now. At first, we kind of just sensed them. Maybe they'd made some small sounds or something, I don't know, but somehow we knew they were there. Then we started catching glimpses of them. Just a peek through the brush, maybe the sound of breathing followed by a swish when we turned. Then we'd just see hindquarters disappearing between the trees. A couple of times I shooed one off with a branch. Just shaking it at the thing and making snarling sounds. I didn't bring a gun. I don't know why I didn't bring a gun. I mean, I'm an anti-gun guy. Big on gun control. But in this situation. No gun. Pretty stupid, huh?

We noticed the wolves getting closer, more aggressive, as we moved toward our destination. Still, they didn't attack. It was almost as if something was holding them back. Like maybe there was some outside force controlling them. That probably sounds crazy. But, we're tracking Dracula, right? I signed up for crazy. But Anica didn't. She had no idea that I was interested in the vampire. Getting her out of here unharmed has got to be my priority.

Anyway, let me give you an example of this crazy wolf behavior. I was walking along and heard this crunch of leaves to my right. When I looked I saw eyes. Just eyes. Iridescent. Staring. Watching me. I stepped forward and the eyes moved with me. I backed up. The eyes moved back an equal distance. I jogged forward. They moved forward, but slowly, no hurry, no rush. Just chilling. I think that was worse. That the wolf didn't increase its pace. It showed a confidence, maybe a purpose. I can tell you, it freaked me.

And this just went on and on. I mean it seemed forever. Every five minutes is a new eternity when you're being stalked. I whispered to Anica about the wolves. She'd never seen this behavior before and was scared pretty much speechless.

Still, we continued on. I mean, what else were we supposed to do? The wolves would be there no matter which direction we walked. At times we thought they'd gone, that maybe they'd lost interest. But then we'd hear that crunch of leaves, or see a sleek gray pelt race by on one side or the other. It felt like… I'm not sure. Like we were surrounded. Like there was this circle of wolves all around us and they just paced us, staying just out of sight. Just waiting. Waiting for something. I didn't know why. Maybe for dinner time. Maybe just to watch. You know, I was looking for rational explanations when there were none.

And they stared. Yeah. They made a thing of staring at us.

Like spies. I know from the documents collected by the Van Helsings that Dracula has used animals as spies before. I'm thinking, maybe he's doing it here. In fact, I'll go out on a limb and…

Wait. What's going on with the fog? Can you see that, the way the fog's following us? It's been doing that for a while now. But now something's…

Anica! Behind you!

Transcript of a text sent by Peter Van Helsing
April 09, 2014

Aunt Lizzy. Come quickly. Ungur Castle. Wallachia. Hurry!

Letter from Anica Dalca (Translated from Romanian by Professor Dalila Nicolescu from the University of Bucharest) April 11-June 7, 2014

Papa,

I don't know if you'll ever read these words. As of this writing, I have no means of delivering this post and our phones have been taken from us. Oh Papa, I fear I have made a terrible mistake, one that may very well cost me my life as well as my soul. But, let me back up. There's a story to tell and I'm hoping that if I can somehow get this message out that maybe the details will help you to reach me before it's too late.

But hear me now, and please—please!—follow my direction in this. If, when you reach me, you find me to be changed, you must kill me. Don't let me continue in some cursed existence. I know I have always been the skeptic and so these words will sound strange to you. But once you've read this account, everything should become clear.

As you know, I was hired by a foreign tourist to act as a guide. The man is kind, a bit peculiar, but well intentioned, and even brave in his own way. What you don't know and what I only realized once we were well into the excursion is that this man, Peter Van Helsing, came to Romania to hunt a vampire. Dracula, Papa. He's come to hunt Dracula.

Now, you know that when it comes to this topic, I'm happy to call people idiots, fools, smallminded, or whatever other insult presents itself. And that's exactly what happened as we made our way up the narrow winding path. I learned of his plan and I scoffed. I ridiculed him just as I have mocked you and Mama. How could I have known that your superstitions were not superstitions at all, but honest to God facts? Oh Papa, I've been so foolish and arrogant. I can only hope that I'll have the opportunity to apologize in person. I know how worried Mama must be, and she's so ill. And I've been insolent, disrespecting her for not being the modern woman

I thought she should be. Please tell her that I love her so very much and regret all of the grief I've caused.

But, I'm rambling and have no idea how much time I'll have to write this and so I'd better get to it. Peter and I were traversing the rugged land up to Ungur Castle when we discovered that we were being tracked by wolves. They followed for some time, simply padding along behind us. Sniffing at the air, gazing through the brush, emitting low almost mournful growls. There must have been at least a dozen of them, maybe more. It was so difficult to tell in that heavily wooded area.

The fog made it all the more difficult. I'm not sure when it first appeared. I guess it must have come upon us gradually. But in the end it was a thick white form that moved almost as a living thing. Papa, this mist didn't follow the breeze, but appeared to act independently, slipping between tree trunks, entwining itself about rocks and brush, creeping along the uneven ground. It came at us from all sides. I know you will recognize the source of this thing because you've warned me of such evil since I was a child. But I must admit that even then, confronted by the truth, I refused to believe that anything unnatural was occurring.

Soon the fog encircled the small clearing we occupied. And then the wolves moved in. Slowly, with teeth bared, heads lowered, eyes glowing red, they padded forward. Closer, closer. Many drooled. Some nearly grinned. Peter knelt, discontinuing his video recording and slipping his pack from his back, unzipping it, and withdrawing four daggers. He gave two to me and then held one in each hand.

Instructing me to stay behind him, he whispered his intent and then, before I could respond, let out a loud yell and lunged toward the nearest, most aggressive, beast. He tried to bury his knife in the creature's neck, hoping that if he dispatched the alpha the other wolves would scatter in confusion and fear. But the wolf anticipated Peter's attack and twisted left, clamping its jaws on his wrist and causing him to drop the blade. He still held the second knife and stabbed furiously with his left hand. The wolf shook its head right and then left repeatedly, causing Peter to stumble to the ground and finally losing his remaining weapon.

I moved forward with the intent of stabbing the wolf before Peter could be mauled but three other beasts leaped forward blocking my way. I moved left. They adapted, stepping to their right. I moved right. They padded forward, lips curled back, teeth bared. One let out a deep menacing growl. Papa, I thought I was going to die.

But these animals did not strike. It seemed their only goal was to prevent me from helping Peter who was being pulled to and fro by the huge alpha. He pounded on the wolf with his fist. At one point it appeared he tried to press his free thumb into one of the wolf's eyes, but the creature was relentless dragging Peter about by the arm as he shouted and pounded on the beast.

But while the wolf maintained its grip on his wrist, it did little damage. There was blood, but only minimally. It wasn't mauling him, but simply subduing him. Peter, wincing in pain, made eye contact with me. "Anica," he said. "Don't attack them. If they'll let you, move away slowly. No quick movements. If they move to intercept you, stop. Don't do anything to anger them." Blood was flowing from his wrist. His voice was strained with pain, but still he instructed me calmly and with authority.

I nodded, but didn't move. I could tell by the animal's posture, crouched as if ready to spring, that they wouldn't allow me to pass. It seemed we were at the mercy of the wolves and it was likely only moments before they decided to make us the day's meal.

It was then that the man appeared. I didn't hear a carriage approach, but this was his mode of transportation. Old. Like something from the eighteen hundreds, a horse drawn carriage. Yes, I know that we still have horse drawn carts in the village, but we also have automobiles and trucks. This carriage, though, was no cart used for hauling wood and hay about but rather an elegant vehicle with fine leather seats, gold trim, and elaborate filigree. The horses were monstrous in size, pure black, and glistening with perspiration. I've never seen finer creatures.

The man, though, was not nearly as impressive. He was short and unevenly formed. It seemed that maybe his left arm was longer than the right, that one knee bulged while the other receded. Maybe this was an optical illusion, but it was unsettling. His white hair spilled over the shoulders of his too-small jacket. His mouth was broad, his lips full, his cheeks puffy and pale. And his eyes, Papa, his eyes were cloudy and glazed. It seemed that though he stared directly at us that he was somewhere else entirely. It was almost as if he spoke to us through a great gulf. I know this sounds silly, but please remember what we're dealing with.

His first words horrified me. "Van Helsing," he said in heavily accented English. "The master has dispatched me to collect you."

Papa, he knew Peter's name. He knew that he was coming. Nothing we had done had gone unseen.

"Come," said the man. "Unless, that is, you would prefer to fill this wolf's belly." There was no joy in his tone, nor was there threat. He spoke fact, nothing more. The man then nodded and the wolf restraining Peter released its hold.

Peter stumbled away, gripping his arm to stay the blood. "I'll go with you," he said. "But leave Anica. She's just a guide."

There was a pause, maybe a slight tick at the man's neck. "No," he said finally. "The master, it seems, might enjoy this one." He then stepped forward, snatching me by my left bicep. His grip was vice-like. I stomped on his foot, punched him in both face and belly. All to no effect. It was as if he felt no pain, that he was disconnected from the sensations of his own body.

Peter made a move for his knife but the alpha wolf stepped forward, placing a near fist-sized paw on the blade. What kind of creatures were these? No natural beast would behave so. This moment may have signaled the first fissure in my oh-so-holy skepticism. Though I was still far from abandoning my rationalism for belief in monsters, I had to at some level become open to the possibility that the world wasn't quite as ordered as I'd hoped to believe. The bizarre behavior of the wolves, the unnatural movements of the fog, the glazed and faraway look in the man's eyes, the idea that he felt no pain when assaulted. I just couldn't process it all. None of it fit my reality.

The journey to the castle was long and nerve-racking. Peter and I were led to the carriage and instructed to sit in the compartment, the man—we learned his name was Lupei—climbed atop to drive the horses. We weren't bound, the doors to the carriage weren't locked, and yet we had no option to flee, for the wolves paced the carriage, never leaving our sight, never straying more than a few feet away.

Peter sat across from me, a look of intense concentration on his dark features. Twice, I attempted to talk with him and both times he shushed me with a quick move of the hand and a rush of breath. He'd wrapped his injured wrist with a cloth and pressed on it with his left hand. Finally, he said, "I've been thinking. I don't have a solution—don't know that there is one, not yet at least—but our first priority is to keep you safe." He paused and glanced through the glass at the trotting wolves. "Dracula knows I'm here. He knows who I am and why I've come. It sucks, but it's the deal. He's fought Van Helsings for over a century. He'll do whatever his twisted mind can think of to me. But he doesn't know you. As far as he knows, you're just some random girl. You're pretty and that might be a problem. Dracula might want you as his own. He might want to vampirize you and make you one of his crazy fang gang brides. We can't let that happen." He narrowed his eyes and leaned forward, elbows on thighs. "What would make you more valuable as a human? He already has a human slave in Lupei, I doubt he needs another. At least not another with the same purpose. What is it you can do for Dracula that no one else can do? Something that you couldn't still do as a vampire? You know, something that can only be done during daylight hours."

I had no response. I'd not yet fully come to accept the idea of vampires, how could I hope to come up with a way to be of value to one? The question was as impossible as it was ludicrous.

"Anica, come on," said Peter. "Think. You've studied abroad. Your English rocks. You've been offered a position in the government. What can you offer Dracula?"

"I don't know. I don't see how any of that can help."

Peter nodded, nearly spoke, but then paused. Again, he looked through the window. "Influence," he said at last. "You can offer influence."

"What?"

"You're educated. You got a job as a speechwriter, right? That means you have connections in government. Offer to take care of Dracula's business matters. He owns property, pays taxes, probably has all kinds of crazy dealings. Business is conducted during daylight hours. Tell him you want to be his right hand girl."

I stared at him as if he was a fool. "I haven't even started at the job. I don't know anyone in the government. What good would I be?"

"Don't you get it? This may be the only thing that saves your life. I can't count on being alive to help you. Let's be honest, Dracula's not a fan of my family. But, you've met this politician guy, your new boss, who is he?"

"The secretary of finance."

"Boom! Perfect. You've met him. Even if only in interviews. It's a connection, a person of influence you can toss at Dracula. Secretary of finance. Nice. Dracula moves within the human world. He has financial dealings. You could be valuable in the business world even if you haven't yet made many connections. But, here's the deal. You probably only have one go at this. You won't overpower him. He's too strong. Like, I don't know, a gorilla or Spider-Man or something. My weapons are gone. He's crafty and powerful. You need to give him a reason to keep you alive and you need to be convincing. You need to sell it. Do you get what I'm telling you? Trash your doubts. Forget about everything else and think of how you can convince an arrogant monster who's been alive for centuries that he can't live without you. Simple, right?"

He grinned then. I almost smacked him.

***

Someone was coming and so I needed to stop writing. Since I've written this on a small spiral memo pad I had with me at the time of my abduction, I've decided to keep it hidden within my bra. I considered hiding it beneath my mattress, but felt this method best if it's to remain undiscovered.

But, Papa, let me continue. We arrived at the castle shortly before dark. Strangely enough, the most disconcerting thing about the place is the constant hum of the large generator that provides electricity to the centuries-old structure. The place was everything I could have expected of a medieval castle and nothing at all of what I would could have anticipated. The structure itself is massive, the walls both interior and exterior are of roughhewn stone. We were led to a large room adjacent the main entrance area. The ceiling there is three stories high with wooden rafters crisscrossing the space. The floor is of polished marble, a massive fireplace takes up three quarters of a wall. Three longswords hang above this on a wooden rack. A portrait of a young woman in what I believe to be seventeenth century dress is mounted to the right of the fireplace. All of this spoke of another time, another world. But there's a seventy-inch television on one wall, a leather recliner before it, a collection of Blu-rays—mostly National Geographic specials and political documentaries—on a rack beside the television. Several brightly-colored photographs of the Chicago skyline hang above an L-shaped couch. This seemed odd to me until Peter explained that Dracula had lived in Chicago for the better part of a century.

Upon entering, Lupei instructed us to remove our coats and to give him any supplies and electronics. Peter protested but Lupei simply smiled saying, "Mr. Van Helsing, we know why you're here and you know that we know why you're here. Let us not play games, hmm? Relinquish your possessions and perhaps we can handle this in a civilized fashion." He looked at Peter long and hard, almost as if he was trying to communicate something nonverbally. After several moments, Peter nodded and began emptying his pockets. Lupei took his backpack before Peter could hope to open it. He'd already taken our weapons, I guess he wanted to make sure he hadn't missed anything earlier.

Papa, I've never been so frightened. I didn't believe in any of this. It was all superstitious nonsense. How could this be happening in a rational world? It seemed all I'd ever believed crumbled in those coming hours. All of my dreams of a better—modernized—life. My career, my planned escape from this backward region. It all vanished. I was a prisoner to a creature that I refused to believe existed. Do you realize how disorienting that is? Nothing—nothing!—was remotely as I believed it to be. I'd lost my bearings, my point of reference. I no longer knew if I could trust my own senses, my own intellect. How could I have confidence in my instincts to get me through this when they'd led me so far from the true and horrible reality of the world?

Lupei nodded continuously and hummed as he collected our belongings, all of the time muttering this and that about the master. "Oh, what would the master think of this." "Better not allow the master to see that." "He might be in a foul mood should he get wind of this." From time to time he would pause, his gaze would change, his expression slacken, and he would glare at Peter. And then it would pass and he'd continue about his task. I wondered about the man, about the hell he must inhabit. Did he voluntarily serve the devil or was he some sort of mind slave? And if a slave, was there anything of the true man left or had Dracula stolen his humanity? Lupei angled his head toward me, his lip quivered, there was moisture in his hazy eyes as he studied me. My God, Papa, it was almost as if he'd read my thoughts, as if he somehow knew what I was thinking about him.

After a moment, he offered a tight grin. "Miss, perhaps you should take a seat? The master will be with you shortly and you might want to relax before he arrives." He indicated a large cushioned chair situated near the fireplace. Turning to Peter, he added, "I suppose you should do the same, but, in truth, I do not hold out much hope for you—Mr. Van Helsing." He then wiped drool from his chin, gathered our belongings, and exited the room.

Peter and I stared at one another, indecision ruling the moment. Should we take this opportunity and attempt to flee, should we pull the swords from above the fireplace to arm ourselves, should we hide? Ultimately, Peter smiled, shrugged, and sat in one of the chairs. "Dracula wouldn't leave us alone if he thought we could escape. Might as well chill while we can."

"What about the swords?" I asked.

Another shrug. "Obviously, he doesn't see them as a threat." He rolled his eyes and chuckled. "Okay. He doesn't see them as a threat in our hands. Guess he doesn't put me in the same league as the other Van Helsings."

I stood rigid. How could Peter give up so easily?

"Hey, hey, hey. I'm not caving in," he said, obviously sensing my mood. "Dracula's confident right now. We'll get our chance. Just be cool."

"And what chance might that be?" The voice came from directly behind me. The English was spoken in a perfect Midwestern American accent.

Peter grinned, nodded, and rose. The man smiled at the most inappropriate times. "Oh, hey," said Peter. "You know. The obvious. A chance to kill you. Or maybe to get away from this place with our lives. I'm shooting for both. Any chance I can interview you for a documentary before we get down and dirty?"

Dracula's face was familiar to me. I had seen it in paintings and on busts for all of my life. Vlad III Dracula, the Wallachian prince, the so-called Impaler. In many ways he's a folk hero in this land. But those who believe in the darker tales whisper of his immortality, of his lust for blood. He is tall, but not exceedingly so. He has the prominent hawk-like nose and full lower lip of his portraits. The eyes are wide and recessed deep into the sockets. His face is gaunt, his cheekbones high and obvious. His hair is the color of midnight, but is now trimmed short in a contemporary cut. He wore a gray woolen sweater and charcoal-colored slacks. His shoes were patent leather, his wrist watch gold. How unlike anything I could have ever expected.

But then there were the fangs. Whatever limited skepticism I'd retained slipped away then. They weren't immediately obvious. I'm sure he long ago learned how to hide them. But when he grinned at Peter, they were on full display. They are odd, in no way human looking, or even mammalian for that matter. To me, they seemed too flat, too tapered, nearly triangular. And sharp. I would guess that they're closer to the shape of a hooked razor blade than anything or maybe like shark's teeth.

"Van Helsing," laughed Dracula. "You are as arrogant as every Van Helsing I've encountered. I must ask, what is it about your family? You fail and then fail again—it's nearly a tradition—and yet you persist in pestering me. Do you people have nothing better to do?"

Peter laughed and said, "Oh, come on. Really? After all that's happened, the defeats you've been handed by my family, and now you rock your ego?" He chuckled but I could see a slight quiver to his hand and the glint of perspiration on his brow. He was putting on a good show of it, but the man was terrified. "Get this. The way I see it, you've either been killed or nearly killed by my family members and/or their companions on three separate occurrences. I know you have some crazy spell that revives you. I've read about that. Something to do with some sort of mystic sorcerer way back when. Nothing you did yourself. You were just scared enough to find someone capable of performing the enchantment. Yeah, that's right—scared. You were terrified you might die someday. A fact that everyone else lives with every day of our lives. And we manage to cope. Something you, oh great vampire, can't seem to handle. So, how is it you keep convincing yourself that you're the big prize winner? If it wasn't for that resurrection spell you'd be dust and bad memories."

There was a flash of anger on the vampire's face, but only for an instant. "Ah. And so the game begins anew. Or rather, perhaps it simply ends. Do you feel, Van Helsing, that you are my equal? Do you somehow presume yourself to be my match, that you will be the one to finally outwit me?"

Peter offered a weak shrug. "The truth? Nah. I just wanted to get some good video, prove to the world that you're real."

Dracula grinned. "Now, now. That is not all. You brought weapons. I believe your intent went beyond capturing video footage."

Peter shrugged. "Yeah. Well, preparing for any contingency. But hey, I'd still like to catch an interview. You'd be a YouTube sensation." Peter offered a twitching grin. Whatever bravado he displayed was a cover. He was terrified. And for good reason.

Dracula nodded. "You are not much of a Van Helsing. Not even worthy to be ranked as an opponent. A pity. Knowing this, I wish you had never come. For this encounter is good for neither you nor me."

Peter's Adam's apple bobbed as he said, "You're a monster. I may not be up to the task but somebody needs to stop you."

"And so you've appointed yourself my executioner? Do you somehow believe that your family heritage has granted you the ability to claim victory over me?" Dracula stepped forward, gazing down on Peter with red glowing eyes. "We have never before met, you and I, and yet you are of the Van Helsing line. Who are you, then? Which Van Helsing was cursed with such a soft and unimpressive offspring?"

Peter met his gaze. "Stephen was my father."

"Ah! Of course. That seems right. You are not worthy of Elizabeth. But, Stephen. Oh, I remember how easily he died. I recall all of the secrets that he so readily revealed." A pause, and then, "Just as I will remember all that you will willingly share."

Dracula cupped Peter's chin in his palm and said, "Are there any final words, any last pleas before you become mine?"

Peter tried to shake his head free of the vampire's grasp, but Dracula's hold was firm. Papa, I don't know why I didn't intercede. In the moment, I couldn't even think of acting. I was transfixed, horrified even. I just stood there and let him do it, Papa. I stood and watched as Dracula leaned forward, whispering into Peter's ear, calming him, stroking his cheek, before finally biting into his neck. Peter never uttered another word.

From the Files of Van Helsing Investigations
April 14, 2014

CASE NUMBER 407

NOTES FROM APRIL 14, 2014

AS RECORDED BY LIZZY VAN HELSING-MULLIGAN

We've been in Romania for six days. Peter's text which instructed us to go to Ungur Castle at first seemed to be the key to finding the man. But Ungur Castle doesn't appear in any literature, not online, not with the Department of Deeds. It was suggested to us that such properties are sometimes renamed when ownership changes. These name changes are not always registered in any official manner, but take place locally. It's in how people come to refer to the property. In other words, if the Castle was known, for instance, as Albescu Castle, and was then purchased by a family named Ungur, it might be referenced locally as Ungur Castle, but still bear the official title of Albescu. And so we spent our first several days in Romania moving from place to place, investigating real estate transactions involving such properties over the past three decades. It was a frustrating exercise. We've had no further communication from Peter and can only imagine that something awful has happened to him since that communication. He's posted no further videos to YouTube, there have been no calls. Nothing.

Our break came early yesterday morning when we entered a small rural village. My son Dane and I are both dark skinned as is Peter. It's obviously rare for someone of our race to venture into this secluded community and it wasn't long before we were approached by a man asking if we were connected to the man who came through here last week. My first impression was that the man might attack us. His eyes were wide and his voice filled with anger as he marched up the narrow lane to meet us. His English was heavily accented, but understandable. "What have you done with her?" he nearly screamed. "My baby, what have you done with her?"

I stepped forward. "Sir, I'm sorry, but I don't know what you're talking about."

His eyes narrowed. He glared at me and then at Dane, ignoring Conner and Kerri. "A gentleman, like you," he said. "Dark. But with bleached hair. He came to lead my Anica away." Anica. I recognize the girl's name from Peter's last video.

Dane rolled his eyes and said, "Smooth," under his breath.

Glancing at my son, I mouthed, "Don't."

He chuckled and shrugged.

I could have been offended at the potentially racially charged comment but, as stated, this was a very homogenous community. The man likely saw few people of color here and so rightly assumed that Peter and I were related. "Sir, we don't know anything about your daughter, but the man that she's with is probably my nephew, the man we've come in search of. Do you have a name?"

He glared at me. I got the feeling he was sizing me up, deciding if he could trust me. "Petre, perhaps. No. Americanized. Peter. The man, I believe, was named Peter."

I felt a flutter in my belly as I glanced to Conner. He nodded and said, "Peter is my wife's nephew. We've come looking for him. Can you tell us where he is?"

"Where he is? If I knew this thing I would know where to find my Anica. Why do you think I come to you like this? My little girl, she is gone and it was this Peter that took her."

Conner offered a subtle shrug. "That makes sense. But here's the thing. We're looking for Peter. He's missing and it's taken us nearly a week to get this close. You say Peter's with your daughter. He was looking for Ungur Castle. Is that anywhere near here?"

The man's eye widened further. "Unger Castle. What could he possibly want with this devil's place?"

I said, "So you know it?"

"Of course it is known to me. It is a three day's journey from here on foot."

"Sir," I said. "We need to get to Peter and your daughter as quickly as possible. There could be danger."

"Nosferatu." His voice was nearly a whisper.

"Bingo," said Dane. "Vampires."

The man, whose name is Serghei, agreed to be our guide. But he warned us that the way was not traversable by car. He might be able to come up with five horses, but we might need to abandon them at some point to proceed on foot. There was no quick way to get to Peter.

We decided that it was too late in the day to begin the journey and so spent the rest of the afternoon and evening in preparation. We oiled our crossbow, coated our knives in garlic oil, and distributed crosses. Serghei did manage to procure the needed horses, but even so the terrain was rough, the going slow. Two of the animals were so old that they couldn't keep the pace even from the beginning. Dane quipped that, "We could hire a helicopter and drop right in on them."

Kerri replied. "I don't think that would be very subtle. Vampires are known to have keen senses and helicopters are noisy."

"Helicopters are noisy. Got it. Thanks for that brilliant observation. That why my parents hired you as an investigator? Quick on the uptake?"

Kerri, in her typical way, ignored the sarcasm and responded to the question directly. "They hired me because of my qualifications: a degree in criminal justice and several months working security at a large property."

Dane chuckled. "What? No vampire hunting? What good are you?"

Kerri smiled. "While I lack real life experience with vampires, I've made a point to study them thoroughly, especially actual documented encounters. Fictionalized accounts have little value."

"Good for you, girl. You stayed away from Twilight. Can't wait to face Dracula while you watch my back."

Obviously, Dane is less than impressed with Kerri. Fortunately, she seems oblivious to his insults and quips. If they impact her at all, she gives no hint of it.

We had to abandon the horses midway through the first day. The road was washed out, nearly undiscernible beneath boulders and fallen trees, the grade steep, the rock and soil loose and subject to shifting. It was clear that we would need to make the rest of the trek on foot. This was disheartening because it would add considerable time to our journey. As well, though Conner and I are in good shape for our age, we are still elderly. This type of travel is very wearing. Our three younger companions distributed most of the gear between them in order to lighten our burden, but still the terrain wore on both of us—though Conner would never admit to this. He's stubborn that way. It would not be exaggerating to say that there was not a spot on my body that didn't ache. It was all I could do to hold back the tears as we moved further and further up the steep grade.

Somewhere near evening we passed a ditch littered with human skeletons. Many appeared undamaged, but there were others with clear indications as to the cause of death: crushed skulls, a sword through a rib cage, shattered bones that were little more than jagged chips of white. None of the bodies were recent, at least not obviously so, but they still served as a warning. Pass at your own risk. Trespassers will be dealt with severely. Kerri allowed a gasp and it appeared she fought down bile. But she contained her revulsion and moved on silently.

An hour later we encountered two men impaled on long coarse spikes, maybe six foot in height and eight inches in diameter. The bodies were barely husks, the birds had pecked most of the skin from the bones, vacant eye sockets gazed at us through eternity and tongueless mouths called a silent warning to any who might pass. Conner eyed me. We both knew what we were heading toward. Despite our history with vampires—or maybe because of it—I wondered if we were emotionally prepared for the coming encounter. Conner still battles with nightmares and I get a paralyzing chill when I think of my brothers, my mother, my father, all slain by this monster. How can I, at this stage in my life, hope to do what our entire family failed to accomplish during our prime?

Serghei allowed a shuddering gasp and Kerri whispered, "Vlad the Impaler," as if anyone was in doubt as to who it was we sought.

"Well," said Dane. "Guess we're on the right course. Special kind of guy, this Dracula, huh?" And then he continued forward. The fear on his face was evident and he didn't want anyone to see his weakness. He's like his father that way, though the two would never admit to any similarities. Conner has a military mindset while Dane's a rogue to his core. Their relationship has been strained since Dane performed his first adolescent acts of rebellion more than two decades ago. Through the years, Conner's experience with vampires has transformed him into a man who believes that the world is too dangerous a place to ever let a guard down. Youthful foolishness didn't fit well with this mindset and so Conner inadvertently made an enemy of his son at a point in Dane's development where he needed his father the most. The tragedy of it is that Conner truly and deeply loves our son. He's just never been able to communicate that love without also commenting on Dane's admittedly bad behavior. He's aware of this and chastises himself after each bout with Dane, but doesn't seem to be able to stop himself when it matters.

Conner is, for lack of a better term, a boy scout. He allows almost no room for error. I've reminded him of his own past drug usage and he says that this is the exact reason he's like this now. He lost a decade of his life to the haze of mind altering substances and doesn't want to see his son waste his life with foolishness. For Dane's part, sarcasm has become his language of choice.

We continued on for another hour even though the sun had slipped to below the horizon. There was no reason to discuss this decision, no one wanted to be anywhere near that scene. We set camp in a small clearing surrounded by mountainous spruce trees that nearly obscured the moon. Our little group was mostly silent with the exception of Kerri who offered an endless stream of facts, detailing everything she knew about Romania and vampires. I'm beginning to have serious fears that Kerri won't be able to keep her wits about her when things get seriously dangerous.

We dined on dried fruits and nuts, each of us sitting about the campfire lost in personal thoughts and fears. I can't adequately describe my state of mind. There was a sense of anticipation and excitement, a hope that maybe we could finally put Dracula behind us once and for all. But that was a tiny voice. Just a whisper. The more predominant emotions were fear and apprehension. How could I hope to face this monster again? How many of our party were we going to lose? Would we—would I—be forced to drink Dracula's blood to become one of his undead slaves? Would I have the courage to end my own life in order to prevent this from happening?

And I felt guilt.

I felt guilt for all those decades ago pulling Stephen back into this life. I felt guilt for giving up on the hunt for Dracula, for assuming—or allowing myself to pretend like I believed—that simply because vampiric activity had gone from Chicago that Dracula was no longer living, or at least active. I knew better. So did Conner. But we were tired. We had a son. We took the easy path and pretended to live normal lives. I know people would tell me that there was nothing wrong with this, that we deserved some peace. But now I think of all of those people that Dracula must have killed in those decades since we last pursued him and the weight of those souls presses down on me. I feel crippled by it. How can I possibly make amends for being so selfish? And how can I forgive myself for wanting so desperately to leave this horrible land, to climb onto a plane and flee back to the States?

Conner sat on a log, staring into the flames. He bent, picked up some dirt from the ground and spit on it making mud. Then he dipped two fingers into the mud and used it to paint a vertical line on his right cheek. He then painted a horizontal line two thirds of the way up the vertical mark to make a cross. He repeated the process on the left cheek. Conner has a strange relationship with faith. He is not a religious man, not in any traditional sense, but he learned, back in the seventies when we fought Dracula, that this vampire is repelled by the cross. Not all vampires are, most, it seems yes, but not all. Still, this led Conner to believe that there is something supernatural about the cross, that God must work through this symbol. And so he has become what I refer to as a faith hermit. He reads the Bible, in particular any passages dealing with evil spirits, he prays in his own fashion, but he is otherwise silent on the topic. He knows that I don't share this belief and he does nothing to sway me. I'm not even sure he would classify himself as Christian or a believer or any other classification. He would simply acknowledge that there are forces beyond our comprehension and leave the rest to interpretation.

Serghei watched as Conner applied the mud to his face and, nodding, pulled on a chain about his neck withdrawing a golden cross from beneath his shirt. I still don't have a solid feel for Serghei. He's in his forties, lean and muscular from his rural lifestyle. He's quiet, but I don't know if that's because his English is not strong, because of his worry for his missing daughter, or if this is just his personality. He's helpful, always carrying more than his share of the burden, but he doesn't mingle with our group. I know he's terrified for Anica and that obviously weighs on him, but I have no words of comfort. None that are true at least. I hold very little hope that we will find either Peter or Anica alive. Despite the stated purpose of this excursion, in my heart I know we're here, not to rescue the missing, but to kill Dracula and eradicate any other vampires we encounter, Peter and Anica likely being among them.

The evening moved into night. We all knew that we must sleep and there was talk of who would sit watch when. But after it was decided that Conner would have first watch, no one moved from the fire. Kerri giggled nervously and said, "Guess nobody's tired, huh?"

No one responded.

It was about a half hour later when Dane whispered, "Ma. Behind you. In the woods."

I turned slowly. At first I saw nothing, but then a ghostly figure, all in white, became visible. It was a female. A vampire, I'm sure of it. Long dark hair, skin as pale as the snow white dress she wore. Her eyes glowed red. She was some distance off, perhaps fifty yards, but I could see her well enough once my eyes adjusted to the dark—I'd been staring at the flames before this.

She made no move toward us, though it was clear that she was watching. I slid a knife from its sheath, Conner reached slowly for the crossbow. Serghei whispered something in Romanian.

The vampire grinned. Even from that distance, I could see that she grinned.

And then there was a commotion from the south. Flashlight beams, voices, the sounds of bodies moving through brush. I turned in that direction and then back to where the vampire had been.

She was gone.

Ten minutes later we were encircled by a group of Romani.

Letter from Anica Dalca (Translated from Romanian by Professor Dalila Nicolescu from the University of Bucharest) April 11-June 7, 2014 (Continued)

Papa, I'm losing track of the days. This is a strange place, a place that seems so separate from any reality I've ever known. I've been given a bedroom to myself but the windows are bricked over. I have no way of knowing if it's night or day. I say bedroom, but in reality it's more of a finely adorned prison cell, for I'm rarely allowed beyond its walls. Lupei is often the only person I see. He brings me meals, but they are at odd intervals which makes it difficult to determine time of day or even when the date has changed. I've questioned him about Peter—who I haven't seen since Dracula attacked him the day of our arrival—and Lupei only shrugs and looks to the ground, sometimes emitting whimpers like a forlorn puppy.

I sense a kindness in the man, maybe even a desire to aid me, but he flees the room whenever I direct our conversation to anything of substance. I know I should consider him an enemy but I can't help but feel that in some ways he might be as much a prisoner as me. Or maybe I'm just being silly. Maybe I'm just so scared that I'm looking for an ally—any ally—even when there are none. What is that called when a prisoner starts to identify with the captor, Stockholm syndrome? Maybe this is some form of that. I don't know. I'm scared. That's the only thing that's for sure. Terrified. Papa, I just don't see a way out of this alive.

I suppose I must tell you about Dracula. God help me, Papa, he is exactly as those ridiculous legends claim him to be. Yes, he is Vlad III Dracula, the once prince of Wallachia now turned to a night demon, I have no doubt of it. So far I've only had two encounters with him, one on that initial day when Peter Van Helsing angered him so and the second during my most recent meal.

Instead of bringing food to my room, Lupei arrived with a long flowing evening gown of a rich deep blue and adorned with black frills. He instructed me to put it on, to do my hair properly, to make myself presentable for the master. When I refused, his face twitched as if he was struggling with something internally. He stepped to me, clasping me by each bicep. "You do not understand," he said. "You have no free will, there is no choice in this matter."

I shook free of him saying, "I'm no one's slave."

He looked to the floor and smacked himself in the head three times. It was as frightening as it was bizarre. I have no idea why he did this, but when he finally spoke, his voice was small and tight. "You are as free now as you ever may hope to be and it is only in obeying the master's command that you can hope to even keep this small liberty you maintain."

"What liberty? I'm a prisoner."

His long white hair had tumbled over his face but still I saw his lips stretch into some approximation of a smile. "No liberty? But you do, young lady. I am certain that you do." Here, he moved forward, his face nearly touching my own as he placed his index finger on my forehead. "You still have liberty of the mind, of your own thoughts. This is a greater gift than you can ever imagine. Now please, make yourself presentable and be the most gracious dinner guest our master could dare imagine." He then took a single step back, bowed, and left the room with his halting uneven gate, leaving me numb with indecision.

Perhaps an hour later, Lupei returned to escort me into the great dining hall where a single place setting was set at a tiny round table dwarfed by the size of the room. Certainly, this chamber was designed to accommodate a lengthy table that could seat fifty or even a hundred people. The little trinket-sized piece looked silly in this great space. Lupei pulled a chair back and motioned for me to sit. As he scooted the chair forward he leaned in whispering, "Do not argue or challenge. Merely smile and nod." He then turned and disappeared through a large double door situated to my left rear.

The table was already set with roast quail, mint jelly, leafy vegetables, some sort of buttered and seasoned potato, and a deep red wine with a yellowed and faded label. I sat quietly, not filling my plate with any of the food, though, in truth, I was nearly famished. Thinking back on it, I'm certain Dracula instructed Lupei to spread out my meals in such a way as to ensure my hunger. Still, I restrained myself, not wanting to appear either too anxious or too cooperative.

The next person to enter the room was neither Dracula nor Lupei but the young woman whose likeness I recognized from the portrait in the atrium. She was, of course, a vampire. Young in appearance, long flowing dark hair, full lips with a saucy twist, a porcelain complexion and eyes to chill the heart of a cobra. "So, this is his current fetish," said the creature as she strolled to before me. "Skinny and weak. Well, he'll tire of you soon enough. He always does." Here she grinned. "And when he does, maybe he'll give you to me. Would you like that, sweet thing? I believe I could offer you a very special kind of hell. Intrigued?" She laughed, low and vicious.

I said nothing, but clutched my fork as one might a dagger.

"Oh, come now," said the vampire. "Certainly, you have a voice." She moved closer and tugged at the front of my dress. "Oh, look at this, look at this. Lupei just doesn't know his task, does he? Show more bosom, girl. Your new master admires young flesh. Let him drool a bit. You might live longer." She leaned in and said, "But when he tires of you, you're mine. Don't ever forget that. Mine to do with as I please." She pecked me on the cheek and laughed.

I was searching for some response that wouldn't reveal my escalating terror when Dracula entered the room through the double door Lupei had used. "Ah! Lavinia," he grinned. "I see you've met our new guest. I'm sure you'll show Anica your every kindness." Here, his eyes narrowed and it was clear that he was sending her a very pointed message.

"Of course," smiled the vampire, though her voice had lost its enthusiasm. "Every kindness."

"Good. Excellent. Then you won't mind offering us some privacy."

"As you desire," said the one called Lavinia as, head lowered, she hurriedly exited the room without a backward glance.

Dracula followed her with his eyes and once the door was closed behind her, turned to face me. "Anica, my dear. Thank you so much for spending your mealtime with me. I have so desired to get acquainted."

I remained silent. What could I possibly say in response? Oh, I thought of calling him a bastard and driving the fork I still clutched through his devil's heart. I thought of spitting in his face. I wanted to scream at him, to demand to see Peter Van Helsing and for the two of us to be released immediately. But what a person so desires to say so seldom resembles the literal words spoken. My only response was to meet his gaze. And, in honesty, I'm proud of this small feat. For he is a powerful personality. His presence fills a room, his will is undeniable. I've never encountered such a force of being. And though he smiled and dressed smartly and acted the gentleman in every way, it was all I could do to control my bladder in those moments.

Seeing that I would give no verbal response, Dracula nodded and slid into the seat across from me. "Ah, yes," he said with a sigh. "You think me to be a monster." He paused. "No. That was a misstatement. Allow me to correct myself. You *know* me to be a monster. And I will not deny it. To refute such a charge would lack integrity. My very existence is monstrous. I feed on the innocent. I have been slain not once but on three separate instances. I rule with little regard for those beneath me. Even in my natural life, I slew viciously and without remorse. Why, should any nobleman in this modern age behave as I once did, he would be relieved of his position and arrested, quite possibly executed. And yet here I sit across from you, a man gazing at a beautiful woman. And I feel that same flutter within my belly that all of your young suiters have surely felt as they approach you with hope for a future and a fear of rejection." He chuckled. "Oh, I am quite certain that you will reject me. How could you do otherwise? If you were to acquiesce to my desires too easily I would know that your motives were deceitful and I would respond accordingly."

He crossed his legs, the right over left, and leaned forward on one elbow. "I'm told the quail is fabulous. You really should eat. And quite frankly, if you do not consume this now, it will be the same food next brought to your chamber several hours from now. Best to enjoy it while it's fresh."

Still, I managed to hold his gaze. "Where's Peter?" I asked with a barely contained tremble.

"Van Helsing? What would you suppose that I should do with the man? He came here with the clear intent to do me harm. He selfishly risked your life by prodding you into his foolish endeavor. What would you suggest I do with such a man?"

"Release him."

He laughed. "Well, who could have predicted that response? Of course you would say release him. But is he truly worthy of such grace? He and his clan have hunted me for over a century. His intent was to slay me. Why should I offer him any less?"

"So, then he still lives?"

Dracula paused, examined his fingernails and said, "I have no interest in speaking of Van Helsing. Too much of my life has been spent avoiding that boorish family. Tell me about yourself. You, I think, are much more interesting."

I nearly lashed out at him. Verbally, that is. I nearly told him exactly what I thought of him and where he could shove his pretense of civility. But then Peter's advice came to mind. It was imperative that I give Dracula a reason to keep me alive as a human. I needed to find some hook, some motivation for him to keep me among the living. After a moment's pause I said, "I'm a native of Romania, but have only just recently returned from England where I attended university. I've accepted a position with the Romanian Minister of Finance."

Dracula appraised me. "Interesting. So you are not a simple farm girl."

"I would submit that few farm girls are as simple as you might assume."

Dracula chuckled.

I continued. "No. I am not a simple farm girl. I hold a position within the government. Admittedly, not a high position—not yet—but one that puts me in contact with important people."

Dracula studied me for a moment and then smiled. "Very impressive. That was your intent, am I correct, to impress me? The question then becomes why? To what end? What is your purpose in seeking to impress a monster?"

"I think that would be obvious. I want to live. Not as some rotting creature of the night but as I am today. A human being who will live and grow old and die one day. I want to maintain my own mind and my own will and I'm willing to use my connections to help you in your business and real estate dealings on the condition that you allow me the life I desire."

"Ha! Oh, brilliant! The girl wishes to bargain."

"Oh, I'm sure that nearly everyone tries to bargain with you, Dracula. The question is, how many of them actually have something to offer? I do. And that earns me at least the opportunity for consideration."

Dracula leaned forward patting the table with his palm. "Smart girl. Clever. Eat your meal. Do not waste. We will talk further, you and I. Yes, we will talk. Now eat, eat." He then rose, winked at me, and exited the room. I nearly fainted from exhaustion brought about by fear and tension.

CASE NUMBER 407

NOTES FROM APRIL 15, 2014

AS RECORDED BY LIZZY VAN HELSING-MULLIGAN

There were more than a dozen Romani. They emerged from the shadows, encircling us. They were mostly armed with firearms, though a couple held long curved blades. I've heard so many stories of the Romani—the

Gypsies—over the years. I know Dracula used many such people as a kind of mind slave when he occupied his Transylvanian castle. And of course there are the tales of their mysterious ways, of their trickery and mysticism. I assumed most of this was racially motivated nonsense and tried to put these preconceptions out of my mind. Let's be honest, most such claims are either exaggerations or outright lies. Though I admit I was apprehensive when I saw the Romani's number. We stood little chance if they proved to be hostile.

Acting as if he was oblivious to the tense environment, Dane stepped forward, a lopsided grin emerging on his face as he spoke to the man who seemed to be the leader. "Hello. Hola. Uh, aloha. Thanks for the save. We come in peace."

Not catching Dane's weak attempt at humor, Kerri whispered, "None of those are the right language."

The Romani stared at Dane as if he was an idiot. I can't say they were wrong. Dane can have his moments.

Fortunately Serghei was with us and stepped to beside my son, addressing the group in the Romanian language. The exchange was short but seemingly heated. When Serghei turned to us and said that the Romani had invited us to spend the night in their settlement, Dane quipped, "Show off."

Conner shot him a glare. Dane shrugged and followed Serghei as he moved to join his countrymen. Unconsciously mimicking my son, I shrugged and followed. We'd just encountered a vampire. There was no telling how many more inhabited the area. Despite any misgivings about the Romani, there was strength in numbers, and they'd obviously found a way to survive in this land. It wasn't a time to be prideful or foolish.

Their settlement was located on the opposite side of the rise we'd just climbed, maybe a mile and a half distant. Men and woman moved about the area, staring at us and murmuring to one another. There were probably fifty Romani in total. Most sat around any of the three campfires. We'd had no idea it was there. How had we been so unaware of them?

We heard laughter and joyous conversation as we approached, but the assembly grew quite as we stepped into the clearing. Most eyes turned in our direction. There were whispers and a young man darted into a nearby motorhome, probably to alert a family member to the presence of strangers. I saw two men pick up rifles and another slip a knife from a sheath. A young woman sat on a folding chair nursing an infant as a toddler tugged at her sleeve. Grabbing her child's hand, she rose, moving quickly to a doublewide trailer. A young boy of perhaps twelve years-old held an IPad up and took a photograph of us as we entered the clearing. He was sitting in front of one of the four more permanent-looking structures, a barn-like home, weather beaten and worn.

Serghei and one member of the small band that had found us moved forward to speak with a man of perhaps fifty who I assumed to be the leader of the community. His beard was gray, his belly broad, and he had a long scar along his right cheek. He nodded and asked a series of questions as Serghei explained our situation. The man's face grew tense and there were more whispers among the nearby Romani at the mention of Dracula.

After several minutes, Serghei turned to us saying, "They believe me when I say to them that these are foolish foreigners here to rescue a loved one from the demon Vlad Dracula."

"Well, I'm glad you made sure they knew we were foolish," quipped Dane. "We certainly wouldn't want them thinking we were in any way competent."

Conner said, "Shut up, Dane."

"Perfect, Dad. Always the supportive father."

The leader, a man named Bavol, marched up to Conner and spoke something in Romanian. Serghei interpreted saying, "He wishes to know what causes you to believe you are able to slay this demon."

Though he spoke to Conner I chose to respond. "My family is well acquainted with this particular monster. My name is Van Helsing and we have slain him twice in the past. We hope to do so permanently this time."

Serghei translated and at the mention of my family name Bavol exclaimed, "Van Helsing!" Obviously, word of my family's exploits had reached this remote village. I suppose it's not such a surprise. These people live within a day's walk of Dracula. They've probably educated themselves on his history.

Making a point to make eye contact with each member of our group individually, Bavol issued a string of harsh sounding words, paused, nodded, and then withdrew to near the fire.

Conner faced Serghei saying, "What was all of that? Are they going to try to prevent us from going forward?"

Serghei shook his head. "No. The opposite, I would say. He still believes you to be buffoons, but they live in fear of the nosferatu. If you seek him harm, it is their desire to aid."

"Really?" said Conner, skepticism in his tone. "They'll accompany us to the castle."

"This, no. The risk is too great. They have, though, offered to get us through the forest alive. They have certain means of evading the vampire. But this is a skill based on stealth, not on actions of aggression. They lead us to the perimeter of the property, no further."

"So, basically, they've offered to deliver us to our deaths," said Dane. "Wonderful."

From the journal of Kerri Rivera
April 15, 2014

So, this is weird. Mrs. Mulligan told me to keep a journal while we're on this case. The Dracula one, in Romania. Until now there really hasn't been much to write about. A lot of nearly identical villages, a very creepy hotel employee (attitude hello!), and some interesting foods—not exactly the kind my travel research led me to believe. I guess written descriptions of food fall short of capturing the true flavor. You could say a taste is worth a thousand words. Cute, huh? See what I did there? So, in short, food: good. Flavor: unusual spices, not too North Americanish. You'll be happy to know that no one's had an adverse reaction to the foreign diet. Which is good because I don't think I'm going to find any quality antacids in rural Romania.

Alright. So, the intro stuff's out of the way.

We're at a Romani camp. Now, you might be tempted to call them Gypsies, but most of them don't like that term because it has connotations. So, I've gone out of my way to be totally PC and use the word Romani whenever possible.

They welcomed us, I guess. I mean they seem a little skittish about foreign strangers baring knives and stakes, but they also seem kind of happy that someone's going after Dracula. There are only a couple of them that speak English, but through Serghei (our guide and translator) they've told us about a lot of strange happenings over the last couple of decades since Dracula bought that castle. Animals being killed or acting strangely, children disappearing, weird women in white appearing in the night to lure men away. It all sounds pretty vampirey to me.

In truth, I've felt like a bit of a tagalong. I've tried to interject with historical tidbits on vampires I've learned through research, but Conner just ignores me and asks the Romani more questions about what they've seen. I guess he feels he can have access to my store of knowledge anytime he wants, while he only has the Romani tonight. But maybe I should put some of my info here so he has access to it whenever he needs it.

So, check out these totally amazing vampire facts:

The ancient Persians were the first to record encounters with vampires.

The vampire Lilith is depicted in ancient Hebrew texts as subsisting on the blood of infants.

There are tales from ancient India of vampires becoming bat-like in form.

The Egyptian goddess Sekmet was, in truth, a vampire. (More on her in a bit, or at least more on her blood.)

A vampire's reflection does not show up in silver-backed mirrors but they can be seen in modern mirrors and they can be photographed. Also, the mirror thing doesn't repel them or anything, it's just a weird little trait having to do with the silver.

During the early nineteenth century there were numerous vampire sightings and encounters in Transylvania.

Okay, that's probably plenty of that for now. More cool factoids to come at you later. I've got tons.

So, remember at the beginning of this entry I said this is weird? Well, here's the weirdness part and I don't really know what to do about it. It has to do with Dane. He's their son, but he's not too much like Mr. and Mrs. Mulligan. He's more, I guess you could say he has his own thing going on. You know, the too handsome for reality, too cool for school, too sly to be Stallone, thing. The worst thing is it works for him.

So, while his parents were talking with the Romani, asking them vampire-related questions, and how best to get to the castle, you know, all of that logistics stuff, Dane was just kind of wandering around, poking his head here and there, eavesdropping on conversations.

Serghei was talking with a Romani named Motshan while Dane was just off to the side, out of their line of sight. Motshan was showing Serghei a small vial of liquid, holding it in the campfire light for him to see. Serghei seemed really impressed. By this, I mean he nodded and smiled and waved his hands around excitedly. They talked for a while and then Motshan gave Serghei the vial. He gazed at it as if it was liquid gold. Motshan leaned in close to Serghei and whispered something. It seemed like it might be some kind of warning or something. Serghei slipped the vial into his pocket and nodded. Motshan hugged him and then patted him on the back. It seemed like maybe they'd made some kind of pact or something.

A few minutes later when Motshan moved away, Dane rushed over to Serghei and asked him about the vial. Serghei said it contained the tainted blood of the vampire goddess Sekmet (remember her from my awesome vampire factoids?!) and that it had the power to kill any vampire. But the problem was that there was only enough blood to kill one. Only one dose. Still, this stuff is apparently like a nuclear vampire killing death juice. If I was a vampire I'd stay clear.

Dane told Serghei that he should turn the juice over to him, or at least to Mrs. M, but Serghei shook his head. Motshan had entrusted it to him alone. It was to be used only if there was a clear chance at killing Dracula with the stuff. You see, apparently Dracula's aware of the vial and this is how the Romani have remained more or less safe. Dracula's afraid of getting doused with vampire plutonium. If the stuff was used on another vampire or spilled or if there was some other misuse, Dracula would feel free to feed on these people. Serghei is to use it only if he has the opportunity. Otherwise, he's to return it to the Romani after our excursion. That is, I'm assuming, that we come out of there alive.

Dane wasn't too happy about any of this. In his mind, something that powerful should be in Van Helsing hands. After all, the Romani have had it for all these years and never found the guts to use it. Van Helsings have actually confronted and killed Dracula several times before. He was kinda right, I guess. But I also see their point of view. The nuclear deterrent thing. They were safe only as long as they had the big bad vamp-killing juice. I really hope Serghei gets a chance to use it on Dracula. It'd be nice to finally get rid of that baddie. And Dane. I don't know. He had this weird grin as he watched Serghei move toward the fire. It seemed like, I don't know, maybe he had something in mind. Like trying to talk Serghei out of it or something. I'm not too good at reading the guy, but something's up.

From the journal of Vlad Dracula
April 15, 2014

Is it possible for a damned soul such as mine love? I have existed for centuries and yet I have no clear answer to the question. Do I have emotions? Quite certainly. I feel anger, grief, longing, sorrow. I know lust and desire. I crave companionship and even, at some level, fellowship. But love? I wish to believe so. And in most ways I would say yes, love. I experience an emotion that might be classified as love, or at the least affection or desire.

But at my core I am a selfish and needful creature. And can someone of that temperament ever claim to truly love another? I believe that I love Lavinia but I found that I could not love her alone. Early in our time together I brought two other brides into our lives despite the pain it caused her. And then, when I chose to relocate to London, I left all three of these devoted females behind. Even after my resurrection I did not return to them for decades.

And now I am here, again with Lavinia, and though she refreshes my soul I find that I long for another. This fragile human girl named Anica. At first I believed her to be a simple peasant girl, but she is so much more. Like Lavinia, her spirit is of fire, her passion sharp and biting. She is intelligent and quick. Her tongue knows little restraint.

I desire her.

Many would claim that my desire for Anica proves that my love for Lavinia is false. And while I can understand the perspective, I propose another line of thought. My desire for Anica has little to do with my affection for Lavinia. Can a man not love two women? Parents love multiple children, why must affection be exclusive? Besides, I have already stated that I am a monster, that I am a being with vast hungers and desires. And so I ask, which would be the greater sin, to give in to my true nature and seek that which I desire, or to ignore my innermost being in order to conform to a moral code established by people that I have never met and who mean nothing to me?

The answer, it seems, is obvious.

And so I went to Anica this night, to her chamber as a suiter to a maid. Her cheeks were damp with tears as I entered. This pained me for I knew that I was the cause and therefore an enemy in her eyes and not worthy of her affections. I sought to initiate conversation, asking about her time in London of how it had changed since my short stay there more than a century past. I asked about her studies, about the young men who surely sought her favor. She responded with perfunctory answers. Short, cool statements, facts alone. I sensed no hint of the vibrancy in her tone.

She then asked about her proposition, about being allowed to leave this place and take her position in the ministry of finance in order to serve me there. When I responded that this would be too great a risk, allowing her to venture into the world beyond, she scoffed, calling me a hideous thing.

Facing her, gently lifting her chin so that she met my gaze, I said, "I cannot change the thing that I am. It is the fate delivered to me. But do not deceive yourself into believing that this is all that I am or all that I can be. For in many ways I am a man as any other man, apparently uncomplicated on the surface but filled with depth and quandaries and desires within. I dream of the many different lives I might have lived, of many hopes long forgotten and of things that might yet be. I ponder the ways of the world and the choices that are made. I question the existence of God and his place in the hearts of the faithful. I long to see a sunrise, to feel that gentle solar warmth upon my skin. Yet you perceive only the monster. Will you not at least attempt to see the man as well?"

She glared at me saying, "You deceive yourself. You might dress well and own property. You might have soothing words, some of which I'm sure you believe. But you are no man and you are not worthy of love. You might be the approximation of a man, but don't fool yourself into thinking that you are any more worthy than a common beast."

My instinct was to lash out, to crush her windpipe in my grasp, to watch her plead and whimper. For maybe then she would realize that she is no different than the deer or the cattle, another thing of flesh to be devoured at my whim. But I am more than the beast she proclaims me to be and so I restrained myself saying, "I accept your incomplete assessment because I know you are under duress. This situation that we find ourselves in, it is far from ideal. But please, grant me a curtesy. Consider my words. You are as an angel brought into a dark land. What I ask is that you shine a portion of your light upon this tarnished soul."

She laughed. Actually laughed at me. "Oh, listen to these words! So eloquent. But still they come from the mouth of a dog."

Dog! She dared compare me to a cur! "Woman, watch your tongue. You do not yet realize who it is you address."

She scoffed. "Ah. And here come the threats. I wondered how long it would take. Not very, it seems."

Insolent woman! How could she possibly have the gall to address me so? "My threats are not idle, dear one. Please consider the restraint I have shown as an evidence of the man within the monster."

"You didn't show restraint to Peter."

Van Helsing. Always she comes back to Van Helsing. "That man is none of your concern. He was no friend to you, but only a stranger willing to risk your life for his own purposes."

"Just as you want me for your own purposes."

I offered a subtle grin, my tone was soft. "I was hoping that we could find a common purpose."

She leaned close, fire in her dark eyes. "Not even in the fires of hell itself will we find common purpose. You are a vile rotting corpse and nothing more. If you want to prove me wrong then let Peter and me go. Otherwise, stop pretending. It only makes you more pathetic."

Never had I heard such insolence. I could not allow this affront to go without response. I could not! And so I pulled her to me. She struggled and cursed as my fangs penetrated the flesh of her neck as I drew her sweet warm life force into my mouth and then into my being.

And she laughed!

Oh, did she laugh. Even through the pain and the fear.

"See," she said. "See the real Vlad Dracula! The mask is gone, the monster revealed."

And then she did the most astounding thing yet. She bit me. Bit me! My mouth was at her neck, leaving my left ear near to her lips. She bit down on the lobe, latched on, pulled, ripped. I howled in pain as she pulled the flesh away. With a bloody grin she spit the flap of skin to the floor. "The meat has gone bad," she said. "Rancid."

Pulling my head back while still maintaining my grip on her, I gazed into her eyes. For several moments we remained as such, each studying the other. And then it was my turn to laugh. "Ha!" I said. "Oh, you are perfect. Just absolutely perfect. I was correct in my assessment. Fire, woman, you have fire."

She kicked and scratched as I then ripped my shirt open, dug into my own chest with long claw-like nails and pressed her already-bloody lips to the open wound forcing her to drink of my blood.

Some fifteen minutes later, when the task was complete, this fiery girl was docile and compliant. A shame, truly. For I had so hoped to harness her verve. But I suppose there was no choice but to extinguish the flame. Some blaze too bright to be tempered. But the loss is minimal and not entirely unexpected. She may not serve me willingly, but serve me she will. And perhaps, with time, when once she has come to understand my true intent, perhaps then her devotion might become genuine.

Upon my return, I found Lavinia waiting in my chamber. "Ah," she said, running her fingers along my damaged ear. "Your new plaything has become more troublesome than she is worth. I'm sure you consider this a pity. But remember one thing always. I am the one bride who came to you voluntarily and I am here still. Remember that and embrace what you have." Here she slipped her gown from her shoulders, allowing it to fall in a bundle to the floor. Naked and beautiful, she embraced me.

CASE NUMBER 407
NOTES FROM APRIL 16, 2014
AS RECORDED BY LIZZY VAN HELSING-MULLIGAN

The trek to Unger Castle took the better part of the day. The path was treacherous and steep and our three Romani guides kept a brisk pace. But they were clearly nervous, whispering between themselves, glancing about wide-eyed, starting at every sound. At first I thought this strange. These people lived here. They knew the area, they probably even knew some of Dracula's habits. But then I reconsidered, looking at these facts through a different lens. They do live here. They do know the area. And, yes, they likely do know some of Dracula's habits.

And this terrifies them.

They've likely found some level of coexistence with this monster, but it must be a delicate balance. They know their boundaries and they know the consequences of crossing those boundaries.

As for our people, with the exception of Kerri—who fed us a near endless stream of facts about vampires and Romania—we stayed mostly silent. We were focused on the task ahead and on the physical challenge of the climb. My body ached in ways I never dreamed possible but I did my best to hold my tongue. We needed to make the castle this day and I feared that if I proved to be a hindrance either the entire party would insist on resting and not continuing until the following day or they would elect to leave Conner and I behind and move on without us. Neither choice was remotely acceptable.

I noticed that Kerri was struggling as well and that she also strained to avoid complaint. Good girl. The stakes are too high. I wouldn't have been willing to wait long for her to recoup. Kerri is not physically fit. She's much more comfortable searching the internet and digging up dirt on cheating spouses and runaway parolees than at climbing up a mountainside to confront a vampire. Though, she does have a certain naïve energy about her that's both charming and disturbing, I really doubt she fully understands what lies ahead.

It was nearly four PM when finally the castle came into view. The Romani warned us that there would be defenses, that there was no possible way to gain entry unnoticed. Having fought Dracula in the past, we'd been prepared for this, but still we were taken aback by the form this obstacle took.

Peter Van Helsing stood before us. Alone. Apparently unharmed.

Though the wind was gusty and the temperature bordering on frigid, he wore no coat but only a silk tuxedo shirt and black formal pants and shoes. From what I'd seen of Peter in his videos—tank tops, bandanas, bongos hanging from his backpack—these clothing choices seemed entirely out of character.

Conner appraised the young man. "Peter?"

My nephew said, "You're Conner and that's Elizabeth." Nodding toward Dane he added, "You are likely my cousin Dane and there's Anica's father. I don't know the others."

Something was very strange. Though I'd never met the adult Peter face-to-face, I'd seen his videos. This man didn't have that same near exhausting verve I'd seen in those, the barely contained frenetic energy that nearly burst from the man. I said, "Yes, Peter. I'm Lizzy. How is it you came to be out here alone and with no coat?"

Before Peter had a chance to respond, Serghei shouted, "Where's my Anica? What have you done with my Anica?"

Peter studied the group, his eyes moving from one person to the next and to the next. When he spoke, his voice was flat and devoid of emotion. "I have done nothing with Anica. In truth, I haven't seen her for some time but I am told that she is well."

"Okay," said Dane. "Anyone else getting the Stepford Wives vibe here? What's with you, Cuz? You and Drac been doing the tiger teeth tango?"

Peter cocked his head, a curious expression on his features, and said, "All is well. I've been instructed to show you to the castle."

Conner stepped to within a foot of Peter and grabbed his head in both hands, studying his eyes, angling the man's face to better see the neck.

"That will not be necessary," said Peter. "I am not a creature of the night. None of you will be harmed so long as you follow instructions. Now, if you don't mind, I would like to move inside to where it is warmer." Peter raised his hands, clasping Conner by each wrist, removing his hands from the face. He then turned and began trudging up the hillside. "I suggest you follow. It is not safe out here after sunset."

Kerri whispered, "There's something wrong with him."

"And once again the girl wins the Captain Obvious award," said Dane who was already moving to follow Peter. "Hey. You guys coming? Drac knows we're here. No way of hitting him with a sneak attack. Might as well play the game, right?"

Kerri said, "That's really not a good idea."

She was right. But so was Dane. No matter what we did, Dracula was going to be one step ahead of us. If we chose to stay out here, he'd likely pick us off one by one using birds or wolves or rats. With a glance at Conner, I nodded and followed our son.

From the journal of Kerri Rivera
April 16, 2014

None of this is good. It's all just—not right. Not what I expected, I mean. I'm in Dracula's castle. The real Dracula's castle. Not that one where tourist go to buy T-shirts and mugs and plastic trinkets but the one he's living in now.

And he's here.

And I saw him.

Dracula. The real Dracula.

But, for the record, I didn't faint or throw up or scream—well maybe a little scream, more of a strangled squeak—but I did get pretty tongue tied. I mean, who wouldn't, right? I knew vampires were real—that Dracula's real—I work for the Van Helsings after all. But knowing something and seeing it are two totally different things.

But, okay. Enough about my near freak-out. Here's what happened.

Peter Van Helsing led us to the castle. Kind of like a zombie pied piper, I guess. He was just quiet and kind of there-but-not-there, just leading the way, silent, never looking back at us. And there were birds following us, like a whole flock of them, just hovering above as we followed Peter through the forest. But they were silent. I mean not a chirp or a caw. Nothing. I don't think I even heard their feathers rustle. Is that even possible? I tried to ask Peter about it, but he just ignored me. Dane pulled me back and told me to stay clear of Peter because he really wasn't himself. I knew this. I mean, it was obvious, right? But I was still hoping he'd respond to a direct question. But he just led the way. Not a word from the man, not a peep from the birds. Creepy as month-old liverwurst.

We were led into the castle and told to wait in a large room to the left of the main entrance. I don't know what you'd call it—a great room, a den, an atrium. Whatever. My apartment's like 800 square feet. I don't have rooms with fancy names. It doesn't matter. For all practical purposes it was a cage.

Peter disappeared around a corner and we were left by ourselves. Just the five of us: Mr. and Mrs. Mulligan, Dane, Serghei, and me. The Romani had remained behind, refusing to follow Peter. No one was really surprised by this. They'd told us they were only going so far. Though, I'll admit, I was hoping they'd stick with it. You know, extra reinforcements and all that. I started to ask Mrs. M what we should do next, but Mr. M shushed me saying, "Assume Dracula or one of his mind slaves can hear every word you say. Stay close to me and don't do anything stupid."

I was about to ask him why he thought I might do something stupid, but saw the look in his eyes. The question could wait for later. Mr. M's really not the kind of guy you want to annoy. He's not mean, but he's not Mister Cheery Pants either. Especially since this whole vampire thing came up. Wow, you'd think someone had just executed his favorite puppy or something. His face just got hard and I'd swear his eyes turned to icicles.

Case in point: the guy was carrying a crossbow. Yeah. A crossbow. He bought it online and had it delivered to our hotel in Bucharest because he knew he couldn't get his own crossbow through customs at the airport. Serious vampire hunter here, that's for sure.

So, there we were in Dracula's castle, just waiting there in some kind of bizarre holding pattern. (The crossbow and all of our other weapons had been collected at the door by a servant.) Dane wandered around the room, just looking at things. There were swords mounted above the fireplace and he picked one of these up and examined it before returning it to its spot. "That thing's sharp enough to kill a vamp. Ballsy of him to leave it where we can get to it."

Mr. M grunted. "He's telling us that we're no match for him. He's right."

"Oh, now that's just wrong," said Dane. "Glass half full, Dad. Come on. A little positivity, huh?"

Mr. M grunted.

Mrs. M said, "Your father's right."

"Then what the hell are we doing here? We could have just grabbed Peter in the woods and been on our way."

Mr. M said, "We're here for Anica as well. It's a rescue mission—for two people. Our objective has little to do with Dracula."

He was right. Kind of. That was the official mission, but we all knew that the underlying goal was to stab that creepy bloodsucker through his sick twisted heart. And so I inched just a little closer to the swords. Who knew, maybe I'd have a chance to skewer the bad boy. I could be pretty quick when I needed to be.

But then Dracula walked into the room and I had the urge to pee.

Intense. I guess that's the best way to put it. Dracula was intense. He had this presence, this aura about him. He didn't do any mind bendy things to me—that I know of - but it felt as if he could reach into my brain and immediately compel me to do whatever he wanted me to do. I didn't like this feeling but I knew it was true. This creature had a force of mind that I'd never imagined.

He was not alone. There was Peter, of course, and another man—the servant who had collected our weapons—who I learned was named Lupei. He was odd in both appearance and behavior. Disheveled, but a little bit classy—is that possible? His long white hair was a tangle, his necktie askew, his tuxedo jacket too small. And as for his behavior, he was like Peter in some ways—zombiefied—but maybe not as much. Or maybe he was more used to it. Maybe he'd been under Dracula's control for so long that the vampire only needed to keep a little bit of mental control on him. Anyway, he seemed more with it than Peter, but not all the way there.

There was one other person there as well.

Anica.

She stood beside Dracula holding his arm, smiling up at him like some dizzy blond from a fifties era beach movie.

Serghei, her dad, looked like he was going to charge Dracula right then but Mr. M held out an arm, stopping him. "Not yet. Trust me. Not yet."

Serghei mumbled something in Romanian. I'm pretty sure they were swear words. That's what I'd be saying if it had been me. But he calmed down—at least a little—and didn't attack yet.

Dracula smiled as if this was all funny. It probably was to him. If I was some immortal crazy dead-but-not-dead creature I might find regular people funny too. But me, I wasn't laughing right then. To be honest, I inched just a little closer to those swords. But even as I did this I recognized just how insane the idea of me—of any of us—killing Dracula really was.

Looking at us with those eyes that had this little flicker of red at the center, Dracula studied us. At the sight of Mr. M, he glanced away, actually averting his eyes. At first I wondered what this was about. Maybe because Mr. M had killed him once back in the seventies. But then I remembered the crosses painted on his face. Dracula was reacting to the cross. But no. He was reacting to Mr. M's faith in the cross—or the power behind the cross. I don't know, but I wished I had whatever it was right then. It didn't repel Dracula exactly, but I could tell it had some effect on him and that was better than nothing.

Finally, Dracula grinned and offered us a greeting. "Welcome guests," he said. Nodding at Mr. and Mrs. M but still avoiding direct eye contact with Mr. M, he added, "Conner and Elizabeth. You've traveled a great distance to see me. I suppose I should be flattered."

I kind of expected Mr. M to throw out some action hero line like, "Don't be, fang face," or, "In your dreams," but he remained silent, clasping Mrs. M's hand and glaring at Dracula, those crosses painted on his cheeks glinting in the flickering light of the fireplace flames.

Dracula nodded. "Of course. We are adversaries and you will never see me as anything but a villain. A shame. We have shared such history, you and I. It would be nice to set our animosities aside, even for a time, to engage in conversation or perhaps even celebration."

"Celebration?" asked Dane. "That sounds dubious."

"Ah. A typical Van Helsing."

"I'm a Mulligan, you dead turd. What do you mean by celebration?"

Dracula smiled down at Anica. "I suppose I should allow my beloved to make the announcement. Tell them, dear. Allow them to share in our joy."

Anica nodded. It was a slow nod. Kind of dreamy. And then she looked directly at her father and said, "Vlad and I are to be wed."

Before any of us could stop him, Serghei charged toward Dracula shouting Romanian curse words. He didn't have a weapon, my guess is he would have clawed out Dracula's heart with his fingernails if he'd had a chance. But Peter and Lupei both stepped forward, each grabbing him by a bicep. Still, he screamed and cursed and clawed. He raked Peter right across the cheek with his nails and Peter didn't even respond. Not even a blink or an "Ouch," even though his cheek was dripping blood. Lupei whispered in Serghei's ear. I couldn't hear the words—and even if I could, they were probably in Romanian—but whatever he said calmed him down some. Not right away. And not completely. He was still angry as snot and I'm sure he would've gone after Dracula again if he had the chance. But he stopped fighting against them and instead stood there glaring at Dracula and snorting like a bull.

There were tears on his face and he angled toward his daughter saying her name over and over.

Dracula said to her, "Perhaps you should comfort your father. He doesn't seem to understand the situation."

Anica nodded and said, "Papa. Vlad is not the creature you believe him to be. You must give him a chance to prove himself. I care for him deeply and cannot wait to become his bride."

Serghei's weeping just got worse. "No, no, no. My sweet Anica. What has he done to you? What has this monster done to you?" I could see him straining against Peter and Lupei's hold again. And for a second, just an instant, I saw something in Anica's eyes. Maybe something like a true recognition. Maybe some kind of new awareness. But then it was gone. Just that fast. Her expression went bland, just blotto.

Dane looked at Dracula and said, "How about you let the lady speak for herself instead of brainwashing her into following your script? Not too convincing when she acts like a puppet on a string."

Dracula grinned. "Young man, I think it best you rethink your situation. You appear to be full of vinegar. Your words are sharp. But may I be honest? Your soul is weak. I hear your heart race. I smell the perspiration on your flesh. I read the terror in your eyes. I applaud your bravado, but let us be clear. That is all it is."

And then he took Anica by the arm and led her away as Serghei screamed and fought against Peter and Lupei. I was surprised that none of the Mulligans tried to stop him. But then, what were they supposed to do? They had no weapons. Dracula might as well have been all powerful. Yeah. We were screwed.

From the journal of Vlad Dracula
April 16, 2014

Serghei, the father, is a problem. Perhaps I was in error in bringing Anica with me for the first meeting with the intruders. Admittedly, it was an opportunity to gloat. And this is a known weakness. My pride has always sought to be unbridled. And, as is often the case, it has led to complications. For instead of displaying my superiority as intended, it has deepened the resolve of my opponents. For now it is obvious that they will not leave without the girl. Even freeing the Van Helsing captive will likely become secondary.

For they believe they know what I have in store for Anica.

They believe that I plan to make her like Lavinia—like all of my previous brides. That I plan to usher her into the eternal midnight. But that is not my goal. My desire is that Anica live beside me willingly and human—for as long as she chooses to remain in that mortal state. True, I have found it necessary to place her within my mental control. But this is a temporary arrangement. Had she not been so strong-willed there would have been no need to implement this measure. But she was stubborn, refusing to accept my affection for what it is. And so I have given her the opportunity to experience my true devotion in order that she might see the error in her rash judgement. But I cannot expect these humans to understand such a thing. Could they comprehend the motive behind my actions? Could they conceive of a monster with the capacity to love? No. They have long ago cast their judgement on me and it is foolish to believe that this attitude might change.

And so the question became this. What to do with Anica's father? For she is an intelligent and willful woman. As such, when we were face-to-face with her father, I could feel her struggling to break free of my mental restraints. And, in truth, she nearly accomplished just that. I found it necessary to exert exceptional mental pressure to maintain my hold on her. And even, then I scarcely maintained control. How was I to proceed?

The solution was offered by, of all people, Lavinia.

As we lay side by side in a bed in the upper chambers, she laid her head on my chest and stroked my flesh with the feather-like touch of her nimble fingers. After several moments she said, "You are troubled, my Lord."

I sighed. "I suppose I am."

"It's the girl. You've not been focused since she arrived. Even your damaged ear has not healed as quickly as it should."

I angled my head to search those so-dark eyes. "You see her as a rival. Of course you would interpret my moods in this way."

Lavinia giggled and stroked my chin. "Oh, Vlad, do not play with me. You know that she is my rival. But there have been other rivals and I expect there will be future ones as well. And yet I remain now and have always held a position of primacy among your brides. And so I hope you will take my suggestions as coming from someone confident in her position as well as from someone who knows you better than anyone else."

She then adjusted, sliding against me, her flesh slipping across mine. And when our heads were one beside the other, she whispered her plan in my ear. A gift of wealth to the father, an offer to grant him a chamber near Anica's own so that he may know that she is well kept.

CASE NUMBER 407

NOTES FROM APRIL 17, 2014

AS RECORDED BY LIZZY VAN HELSING-MULLIGAN

I have never felt so lost, so inadequate. Throughout my life I've been the strong one, the no nonsense woman who wouldn't be pushed around, who dealt with loss and tragedy, who literally embraced dangerous situations. Some people even referred to me as badass. I'm not saying that I never had any vulnerabilities or that I was uncaring. No. I don't believe that either of these was ever the case. But I can also say that I never felt weak. And I know I never felt helpless.

The way I do now.

Conner has always felt the same way. He didn't say as much about his fears, but he didn't need to. I know this because we've been together for nearly forty years. We've never needed to talk in order to communicate. A man of few words but of deep emotion, others have often mistaken him as angry or even cruel. But that's never been Conner. What they saw was simply the defensive skin that built up over a lifetime of tragedy and brutal conflict. I've been blessed to know the Conner within. The kind and generous person, the caring husband and troubled father who had never quite figured out how to connect with his son.

But we both changed with time. Where we were once driven by fierce determination, where we sought to rid the world—or at least our corner of it—of vampiric evil, we stepped away from that life. We bought a house, raised a son, attended school functions and mailed Christmas cards. We tried to pretend that the world that had dominated our earlier years would never intrude on us again.

And now that it has, I've learned how woefully inadequate I am to the task.

Conner and I were given a room together. Dane, Kerri, and Serghei were each given individual rooms. The doors were locked, making us prisoners. Conner sat on the floor in a corner praying for over two hours. Just sitting there, murmuring, glaring at the floor. I wanted to sit with him, to comfort him, but didn't want to intrude on his private time with the deity he simultaneously acknowledged and denied. Eventually, though, I think he sensed my need and came to me, wrapping me in his arms and resting his chin upon my head. He was silent, but the physical contact conveyed his emotions.

It was sweet, precious even. I felt our connection, our shared love. I felt his strength and his vulnerability. And I felt his deep unyielding love for me. I'll remember that embrace for the rest of my days.

The windows were boarded over and so we couldn't see sunlight, but Conner wore a watch and as dawn approached he moved to the door, examining it. "The vampires should be in their coffins by now. I don't know how many human servants Dracula has, but we know of three: Peter, Anica, and Lupei. I'm assuming they'll be keeping an eye on us. Or, at least Lupei will. I don't know if he'd trust Peter or Anica to use force on us."

I foolishly agreed, still unaware of what this horrible day would bring. I said, "Dracula claims to have feelings for Anica. He'll keep her out of harm's way. And Peter, he's just a pawn to use against us. Though I don't think Dracula would give Peter free reign. There'd be too great a risk that we'd influence him."

Conner slid his fingertips across the door handle, his mind already occupied by another problem. "I think this lock can be picked but I need something long and narrow." He glanced around the room. There was a bed. Nothing else. No chairs with legs that could be broken and used as stakes, no end tables with screws and metal connectors that could be fashioned into tools. Dracula hadn't wanted to give us potential weapons.

"Or," I said. "The hinges are on the inside of the door."

"Yeah. And?"

"It's an opportunity. We could remove the door."

Conner grinned. "Not exactly subtle, but yeah. Since it's very unlikely we'll find something narrow enough to use as a lock pick, that's doable."

We needed some sort of wedge to push the pins free of the hinges. As the room was nearly barren, we were forced to seek a solution on our clothing. Conner's belt buckle. It wasn't quite ideal—not really as narrow as we needed—but with effort he was able to wedge the side of the buckle against the pin and strike it with his palm. But with each strike, the buckle slid out of place. I could see Conner becoming frustrated at each failed attempt and so I offered to give it a try. But this just made him angrier.

Eventually, he threw the belt to the floor with a curse and marched away from the door. I gave him some space. He needed to blow off steam. I wish I'd just let it be. I wish we'd just stayed in the room, that we'd never made our way beyond that door. But that was never our way. We'd face every problem head on, never give an inch. Well, that sounds great until you come up against something you just can't beat.

I picked up the belt, moved to the door, jammed the buckle at the intersection of the pin and hinge. Instead of angling the buckle upward as Conner had, I hammered it straight in, using the heal of my hand as a hammer. The pin didn't move, but neither did the buckle slip away as it had for Conner.

I hit it again. And then again. There was movement. It was slight, but the pin had raised just a hair. I hit again. Now there was room enough to squeeze the buckle into the growing space. Another hit, another fraction of a budge, and I was able to angle the buckle upward. Three more hits and the first pin was free.

I called Conner over. I'd need his help steadying the door as I freed the remaining two pins. It took another ten minutes or so, but we eventually pulled the door from the frame.

Conner peeked around the corner to make sure the adjacent hallway was unoccupied and then signaled me to follow. It was foolish. We were unarmed and unfamiliar with the layout of the castle. We had no idea how many mind slaves Dracula commanded or what other traps he might have set. But we'd both always abhorred inaction. We were following our instincts as if they were infallible.

I knocked on the next door to our right, whispering the names of our companions. My hope was that we'd all been deposited in the same area. But there was no response from that room or any others in close proximity. As we were situated toward the end of this corridor, we moved up the hall. I felt naked. We had no means to defend ourselves. What could we do if confronted by one of Dracula's servants?

We took the first left turn and knocked softly on the doors as we had in the first corridor and were greeted with the same result. We continued to the next intersection. I'd never been in a castle before and was surprised both at the bigness and smallness of the thing. It was sprawling, with dozens upon dozens of rooms, and corridors, and offshoots. But the walkways were narrow, perhaps half the width of a typical hotel hallway and the ceiling was low. Not so low as to make us crouch, but probably no higher than six foot six at the highest. There was electric lighting but it was dim and the bulbs tended to flicker frequently. We knew that there was a generator on the grounds that provided the power and assumed that it delivered an uneven flow of electricity, thus the flicker.

The architecture was ornate with fine craftsmanship. The half columns spaced evenly along the walls were adorned with intricate filigree. The floors were tiled with exquisite tiles of brown and red. There were archways spaced about every hundred feet down each corridor. The building itself was magnificent. But it was barren. There were almost no furnishings, no portraits or other artwork along the walls, no plants, no signs that the place was occupied. The castle was as soulless as was its owner.

We were approaching a winding staircase when I saw a shadow move to Conner's right. I'd seen it too late to warn him, but he sensed the movement and, with a surprisingly quick pivot, turned to face the adversary.

It was Kerri.

Conner had already begun to throw a punch when he realized who it was and barely stopped his fist in time. The poor girl looked like she might faint. “What are you doing here? How did you get out?” asked Conner in a near hiss.

Kerri lifted an arm extending her index finger as a teacher might when giving a lesson. “I unscrewed the door handle and then reached in and released the mechanism.”

“You what?”

“The door handle was held on by two screws. I broke a piece of flat metal off of the caster on the bed and used it like a screwdriver.” Despite the slight tremor to her voice, it was clear that she was quite proud of herself. Obviously, the girl brought more to the table than I would have thought. Good for her.

“Have you seen anyone else?” I asked. “Dane, Anica, Peter, Serghei?”

“Nope. I’ve been looking. But I’ve also been kind of hiding.”

I nodded. I certainly couldn’t fault the girl for using caution.

“Any sign of Lupei or any other Dracula cronies?” asked Conner.

“No again. Just me. And now you.”

Conner offered an affirmative grunt. “Well, that’s encouraging. Maybe there aren’t any others. That would simplify our task.”

“It would,” I said. “But we can’t count on it. Our best chance is to keep moving and find the others. There’s strength in numbers.” I squeezed past Conner and Kerri and led the way down the corridor. It may have appeared that I was confident and in control—that was certainly my intent—but the truth of the matter is that I was terrified. Strength in numbers. Sure. It sounded great. And there was a grain of truth to it. But we were unarmed and facing vampires in their own dwelling. How could we have had any expectation that things would end without tragedy?

We found Dane maybe fifteen minutes later. He’d not yet escaped his room and, speaking through the door, we coached him on how to use his belt buckle to dislodge the hinge pins. Upon exiting the room, he looked at Kerri and said, "Oh, you decided to rescue her before your own son?"

Kerri offered a touch of a grin and said, "I freed myself. No rescue needed—unlike you."

Dane simply glared at her. But we didn't have time for damaged egos so Conner told him to suck it up and get in the game. Dane then redirected his glare at Conner and marched on ahead. I wish so much that I'd done something to bring them together in that moment. While there was still a chance. I know they loved each other. But neither seemed to know how to show it.

And now…

Well, now is no time to dwell on it. I must record the events, make sure that there's a record of what occurred. I can deal with my emotions later.

Our next encounter was not with one of our own. We were moving slowly from one corridor to another, opening unlocked doors and whispering through those that were secured. It was risky, and we knew this. There was just as good of a chance that we'd alert one of Dracula's fiends when we called through the wooden partitions as we were of locating one of our party. But we simply didn't know what else to do. Serghei was still unaccounted for and we'd yet to rescue Peter or Anica.

Lupei wasn't lurking behind a door or crouching in shadows, but had just exited a room and was making his way up the corridor carrying a food tray when he discovered us. His first response was of obvious surprise. His hazy eyes widened, he muttered something in Romanian, and then, switching to heavily accented English, said, "No, no, no. You must not do this. The danger. Do you not realize the danger?"

And then his expression changed, hardening as he examined us. His jaw tightened, his eyes narrowed, his lips curled into a twisted sneer. It was almost as if he was a different person altogether. Snatching a steak knife from the plate he then let the tray drop and rushed toward Conner, knife raised, a howl that may have been rage or might have been agony bursting from his lungs. Conner dodged the initial assault, but Lupei, with surprising agility, twisted, slicing Conner across his right side just below the ribcage.

I lunged onto his back. He bucked like an unbroken horse, nearly throwing me to the floor, but somehow I maintained my grip. Conner was still getting to his feet, Dane punched Lupei several times in the face, and I clung to the man's back, arm wrapped around his neck in an attempt to strangle him into unconsciousness, but the man was like a wild beast. It was almost as if he felt none of it.

Until Kerri took the discarded metal tray and, swinging it like a baseball bat, slammed Lupei across the side of the head. He staggered. She repeated the move, this time striking him on the opposite cheek. And Lupei stumbled to the ground unconscious.

I scrambled off of his back and to Conner who was upright but leaning against a wall breathing heavily. "I'm alright. I'm alright," he gasped. "The cut's not deep. Just give me a minute to catch my breath."

"Let me see," I said, pulling his hand away from his side, lifting his bloodied shirt and examining the wound. He was right. It wasn't deep enough to have damaged anything internal, but it was long and it was bleeding heavily. "Kerri, hand me that napkin," I said pointing toward the spot where Lupei had dropped the tray. The napkin lay amidst spilled food, scattered silverware, and the jagged remains of a plate. She did as instructed and I pressed the silky fabric against the wound. "You'll be okay. But we need to stop the bleeding. Keep pressure on it."

Conner put a palm over the napkin and pressed. I wished we had something to use as a wrap, something that could secure the makeshift bandage to his side, but this would need to do.

And then our eyes met and I saw the fear and pain within. So rare for Conner who had learned to harden himself for tasks such as these. I leaned forward, allowing my forehead to rest against his, and whispered, "Conner, sweetie, are you alright?"

He hesitated, swallowed, and whispered, "I'm scared."

I nearly cried. In all of our years together I don't think I'd ever heard him utter those words. I pulled him into a hug. "It's alright, sweetie. It's alright. We'll get through this together. We always have."

He nodded and kissed me, but I could tell that he wasn't convinced. Neither was I, but what choice did we have but to continue forward?

"Hey, guys. Not to intrude or anything, but we need to do something with this Lupei guy before he wakes up." It was Dane and he was correct. We didn't have the luxury of time.

Conner gave me a final kiss and then broke away from my grasp, still pressing the napkin to his side. "Lupei came from that room three doors up and to the right. He was carrying a tray with the remains of a meal. There's probably someone human behind that door. Kerri, check it out for me, will you?" Kerri nodded and did as instructed. Conner then moved toward the fallen man. The side of Lupei's face where Kerri had struck him with the tray was swollen and red. He was still soundly unconscious. Conner chuckled. "Remind me never to get that girl mad at me."

A moment later Kerri came rushing down the hallway. "It's Anica. She's in that room. Anica's in there."

I nodded. "Good. Conner and I will go to her. You two bring Lupei to the room."

Dane cocked his head. "Really? That's my job here? Lugging refuse?"

I snapped my head in his direction. "You and Kerri are young. Your father's injured. Just be useful—okay?" I turned, and moved toward the open door, Conner at my side.

We found Anica in the room, seated on the bed, staring forward. It almost seemed she didn't notice us enter the room. Long dark hair, high cheek bones, large brown eyes, she was a pretty girl, not gorgeous like some model in a magazine, but better. That natural down home type of beauty that is cute and appealing but not dauntingly obvious. Anica had the kind of looks that made people—men and women alike—immediately take to the person. Apparently that trait extended to vampires as well. I couldn't blame

Dracula for desiring her. But I could blame him through eternity for imprisoning her.

She didn't respond when spoken to. Both Conner and I tried to get through to her, but she simply stared. The bite marks were obvious on her neck and she was extremely pale. I heard Conner hiss, "That bastard," as he patted her on the cheek attempting to rouse her.

Dane and Kerri entered the room then, each clasping one of Lupei's ankles, dragging the unconscious man behind them. "Special delivery," chimed Dane. "Who ordered an unconscious douche bag?"

Glancing in their direction, I said, "Find something to bind him."

Dropping Lupei's leg, Dane made an exaggerated act of glancing about the near barren room. "With what?"

"I don't care. Your belt. Anything you can find."

"Forget it," said Conner. "Dane's right. There's nothing here that would do the trick. And by all logic, Dracula will know exactly where to find him and free him anyway. It's obvious there's a strong mental connection between the two. Our best bet is to keep moving. We'll take Anica with us and continue trying to find Serghei and Peter."

"If Dracula can locate Lupei through their psychic connection, can't he do the same with Anica?" asked Kerri.

Conner nodded. "Maybe. But her connection is more recent. I'm hoping it's not as strong."

"Hoping?" said Dane. "So we're taking her with us when she may or may not be a homing beacon for Dracula to find us?"

I said, "We can't leave her here to be Dracula's slave. We'll have the same issue with Peter when we find him. We'll just have to risk it and improvise as we go."

"Well, glad to know you experienced vampire hunters have a solid plan. Ever wonder why I never wanted to join your little Scooby gang before now?"

Conner grunted. "Well, aside from the fact that we quit when you were very young, I was always under the assumption that it was because you were too busy being a smartass to do anything useful." He then marched toward the doorway.

I hated the dynamic between my husband and son. There was love between them, but God in heaven, neither would dare be the first to show it. "Kerri," I said. "Will you guide Anica? In my experience, in this near catatonic state, if you just lead her by her arm she should comply."

"Of course, Mrs. Mulligan." And then, after a pause. "Are Dane and Mr. M alright?"

"They're fine, Kerri. This is actually one of their better days."

I spoke with Anica as we moved through the corridors, asking her questions about her father, about Dracula, about her studies at the university. Anything to try to coax her into a more coherent frame of mind. She was pale and very weak. I knew she needed a blood transfusion to replace what Dracula had taken, but that wasn't something we were equipped to provide. But despite her weakness and obvious mental connection to Dracula she became more coherent as we moved through the building. I believe the activity helped to reconnect her to the physical world around her. Soon I was asking her questions about the layout of the castle, where we might find Peter, where Dracula and any other vampires might be sleeping.

She said that she'd only seen Peter twice since coming to the castle, the most recent was the same time we'd seen him just after we arrived. My assumption was that Dracula kept him on a different floor or even another wing of the castle as he didn't want these two recent additions to his household influencing one another against him.

We knew from previous encounters that Dracula tended to rest in basement areas where there was no chance of exposure to sunlight and so, lacking any solid leads, moved to the lower levels of the castle with hopes of gaining access to the vampire while he slept. Still checking doorways and offshoots as we went, it was over a half hour before we had worked our way down to the main level. Conner and I were fairly well exhausted, Anica was still in a semi daze and Dane and Kerri were each wide eyed and cautious. Arriving at the large room where we'd first encountered Dracula, Conner and I sat down on a couch to rest ourselves as the younger members of our group wandered about peering this way and that, essentially continuing the search. There were arch-shaped windows across one side of the room, they were narrow and about four feet in height. Sunlight eked in through these but they were too small to afford a view of the grounds without moving to within a foot or so of them. Kerri was the first to do so.

I heard her gasp and moved to the window to see what had startled her. I hadn't realized that Anica had followed me over until I heard her piercing scream.

Her father, Serghei, was impaled on a long jagged pole on the front lawn.

The scene was gruesome. Serghei hung face up, the pole entering in the lower back and exiting at mid-chest. His eyes were wide and sightless, his arms hung palms up in a way that seemed almost as if he died pleading for relief.

He probably had.

Dane rushed to Anica, putting a palm over her mouth in an attempt at quieting her. But she shook free. Whatever spell Dracula had placed on her was broken by her grief.

And then it happened.

Likely alerted by Anica's outburst, Peter entered the room. We were all distracted, everyone facing Anica, trying to calm her. Peter moved quietly, unnoticed. His knife slid into Conner's back. My husband screamed as Peter twisted the blade and then jerked it upward tearing through Conner's internal organs. Our eyes met for the final time. It was only an instant before he slumped to the floor dead. But I saw through his pain the immense love he still held for me and I'm certain that my name was his final utterance though it was barely more than a gasp.

Shouting, "Dad!" Dane tackled Peter as I raced to Conner. Kerri dove onto Peter's knife arm, wrapping both of her own arms around his and preventing him from stabbing Dane as he had Conner. But before anything else could happen, Lupei entered the room. He was carrying a shotgun. It was over. But I didn't care. And I'm not certain that I care even now. Conner is dead. My husband. My soulmate. What else could possibly ever matter?

From the journal of Vlad Dracula
April 17, 2014

I glared at Lavinia, screaming over and over, "What have you done? This was not the plan. This was not what I agreed to!" And yes, how could she have done this thing? What gave her the right to trounce upon my will and my designs? She has slain the girl's father, impaling him as I might have done in my human days and thus leaving the impression that it was I that had done the deed.

Lavinia smiled. The audacity of the woman! Though I was enraged, she offered nothing but a haughty grin. "I have done you a favor," she said as she strolled casually toward me, her attitude one of confidence, possibly even arrogance.

"A favor? The girl will believe me to be the culprit."

"Of course she will. And finally you will recognize how utterly she despises you."

I slammed a fist against a wall breaking one of the stones into several pieces. It crumbled to the floor, pebbles and dust, as I screamed, "Of course she despises me. She now believes I have slain her father!"

Lavinia chuckled. "She has despised you always. But you've ignored this, instead behaving as an adolescent with his first crush. You are too blind to see that she can never willingly be yours the way I have been. Do you not recall that I came with you when I was yet human? That I truly desired you?

That I freely allowed you to bring me into the eternal midnight? I stood guard by your grave for all of those dark decades while your ashes lay in the tomb of your enemy. I waited faithfully for nearly a century as you lived across the sea in the new world. And I have stood by you faithfully as a lover and a servant since our reunion. And yet you find a pretty young face and now I am nothing but a servant. She does not deserve you. She has not earned a place here. And she will forever reject you. I have done you no wrong, my prince. I have only sought to awaken you to the foolishness that you pursue."

Insolence! Audacity!

She approached me, a broad smile creasing her lips, a knowing glint in her eyes. She truly supposed herself to be my equal. She actually believed that she could teach me or change my course.

As she stepped to within reach I grasped her neck. "You think much too highly of yourself, Lavinia. You have never understood my needs or my whims. True, you have proved faithful, but so too do dogs if they are fed and kept. But dogs, you see, in the end, must always be put down."

With this I crushed her windpipe, slashed her neck open with my talon-like nails, and hurled her from me. I could hear the moist sucking of her opened throat as she pressed her palm against the gaping wound, but could not stay the flow of blood from the opened vein. She gasped and gawked, her eyes pleading with me for salvation, but I turned from her and allowed my heart to ache as I listened to her agonized gasps.

I summoned Lupei, instructing him to stake her by hands and feet on the grounds where the next day's sun would finish the deed. For this wound was not fatal to one such as her and I wanted her death to be long and excruciating. I will not claim that I felt nothing for Lavinia. The truth of it is that I did love her. And yes, all that she claimed of her devotion was true. But a vampire's needs are great and she was never of the same station as I. In the end, Lavinia did not know her place. It is regretful that I was forced to eliminate her. But this is the way of life. Many things are regretful. One must grow strong against weakness in the face of loss. I will miss Lavinia, most assuredly. But I shall also redouble my efforts to win the fair Anica.

From the journal of Kerri Rivera
April 18, 2014

Mr. Mulligan's dead. I guess it's no surprise for you to learn that I'm in shock. I mean, I knew we were coming to Dracula's castle. I knew there would be vampires. But, call me naïve, but I never really considered the idea that one of us might actually die. Sure, yeah, intellectually I knew this could happen. I'm not stupid. But knowing it in the abstract and actually seeing it happen, not the same thing in any world that I frequent.

I wasn't the only one too freaked out to act. I think we all were. Mrs. M is the most experienced of any of us and she just fell to her dead husband's side. I don't think anything else mattered to her then—not even that we were all recaptured. Truth is, even now, I don't think anything matters to her. It's almost as if all the light in her went out with Mr. M's death. Just poof! Gone.

Dane just stood there gawking at his dad, his jaw quivering. I know the two had their issues, but the guy looked like someone had just put him through electroshock therapy. I felt horrible for him, but couldn't think of anything to say that would be adequate. I don't think there really is such a thing.

Lupei instructed Peter to guard us with the gun as he retrieved several lengths of rope and then proceeded to tie us each to wooden chairs he'd gathered from the dining room. He was all twitches and drools, slapping his own head, muttering. It was like he was having some sort of battle with himself. Very creepy. Thinking back on it, we might have been able to overpower Peter or distract him enough to force the gun from him during that time when Lupei was in and out of the room. But, yeah, pretty likely one or more of us would have wound up dead and, let's face it, I'm not that heroic and everyone else was spun out with grief.

Here's the weird thing.

Lupei didn't tie the ropes all that tight. I know he didn't for me and based on what happened later I don't think he did on anyone. He's a weird guy, Lupei. Kind of back and forth. Sometimes—most of the time—he seems like he's totally Dracula's guy. But then there are times when I think I see glimpses of the real Lupei peeking through. The one that's not under Dracula's spell, the one that never in his life would have willingly served that dirt bag. It's a look in his eyes, a softening, a helplessness, but also a determination. Kind of a weird combination, but that's my not-so-professional take on it. But the short of it is, he didn't tie us all that tight. And he was muttering to himself, almost like he was having an internal argument. And when he was done tying me to the chair, he looked at me and there was moisture in his eyes. And then he patted me on the shoulder and moved on to Anica. God, I almost wanted to hug the guy and tell him everything would be alright.

Then came the long stressful can't-we-just-get-this-over-with part. For, after we'd all been more or less secured, we waited. For hours—long into the night. Peter and Lupei standing guard. Just waiting for Dracula to enter. I pretty much assumed we were just waiting for our execution—either fang bites to the neck or impaling. I couldn't figure out which I feared most. I guess impaling, because it's a horrible death. But then, with that, once you're dead you're dead, where the fang thing could get into that whole undead vampire living corpse thing.

So, as expected, Dracula did eventually make his appearance. The whole scene was strange. Or, if I want to be literary about it, I could say, "oddly surreal." But, no. We'll go with strange. It was just strange.

Dracula didn't come in with vengeance on the brain. He didn't berate us or demand our allegiance. Instead, he went to Anica and kneeled before her, an expression of pained sorrow on his sharp bone-like features. "I am so sorry for your loss," he said. "It was not I that did this horrible thing to your father and neither did I order it. The heinous act was perpetrated by my former companion, Lavinia. And I can assure you that I have disposed of her. She will never trouble you again."

I don't know what kind of reaction Dracula expected, but I'm sure he didn't get the one he wanted. Anica screamed, "You filthy murdering bastard! You killed my dad! Rot in hell! Just rot in hell!"

Dracula tried to calm her, he tried to explain whatever it was he was trying to explain, but she just cried and screamed and kicked. And I could see Dracula's face becoming taut and the anger rising in his eyes. "Woman!" he screamed. "Have you not listened? I am not the one responsible for your father's death."

She spit on him then, or tried to, it fell short and mostly landed on her own shoe, but, as cliché as this move was, she got the point across. Dracula was suitably pissed and I really thought he was about to rip her head from her neck. He probably considered this, but I saw him composing himself, attempting to bring it down. After nearly a minute, he again tried to reason with her. "Anica, beautiful Anica," he said. "Do you not see that I want only for us to live in happiness together?"

She screamed and cursed, both in English and Romanian. She tended to float between the two as did Dracula. She called him a rotting, festering, abomination. She described in detail what she would like to do to his dismembered body.

I could see that Dracula's anger was rising. He held Anica's chin in his thick paw-like grip. His face was only inches from hers. He hissed at her, saying that all he wanted was a peaceful life together, to live away from the conflict and grief. She squirmed, attempting to pull free of his grasp, but he was strong, really strong, and she was more likely to injure herself than to break free of that iron grip.

"You will be with me," said Dracula, his voice becoming almost hypnotic. "One day you will do so willingly, but today? Yes, today too much has gone afoul for you to behave rationally." His eyes. Those deep-set eyes. He was staring directly into Anica's eyes, maybe into her soul, communicating to her, bringing her back under his control.

And then I caught sight of movement to my right. Dane. He was working free of his binds. Lupei had not tied his very tight either. I shook my head, just slightly. I mean, the last thing I wanted to do was to draw Dracula's attention. But I didn't want Dane to do anything stupid. He was unarmed and the vampire was right there. What could he be thinking that he could do even if he did get free?

But Dane just gave me one of those winks of his. He winks a lot. Usually it means he thinks he's about to do something brilliant.

The problem is, Dane's not brilliant.

I glanced toward Dracula, then back to Dane, then to Dracula. The vampire was still trying to win the girl of his creepy undead dreams and not paying attention to us. Dane was really close to wriggling his arms free. I mouthed, "No!" to him. The brat winked again. I glanced over to Mrs. M, but she had her head down and eyes closed. She wasn't asleep, but since Mr. M's death I'm pretty sure she'd pretty much just checked out mentally. I don't really think she cared if she lived or died just then. She was simply too deep into her grief to respond in any healthy way.

Dane's binds were practically falling off. He'd be free any moment. I was sure he'd get himself killed. Yeah, Dracula was distracted by Anica, but he wasn't clueless. He'd see the movement as soon as Dane stood. I had to do something—anything—to cause a distraction, to give Dane a chance.

Shifting right and then left, I toppled my chair.

Dracula turned toward me.

Dane practically sprang free. I was actually kind of impressed by his speed. I mean, he's a normal middle-class thirty-something year-old dude not some CGI enhanced movie superhero. But the move was pretty slick.

I screamed at Dracula to keep his attention, but he sensed Dane's movement and turned toward him just as Dane was almost upon him. This was it. Dane was about to die. This was a normal unarmed guy against a legendary vampire. There just wasn't any other possible outcome.

Except there was.

Because Dane wasn't all that unarmed. He somehow had obtained the small vial containing the toxic blood of the vampire goddess Sekmet. Serghei had had this! How had Dane put his mitts on it? He smashed the vial against Dracula's left cheek, shattering the glass into a zillion shards and sending the ancient blood spilling across the vampire's face. As you might expect, Dracula roared in pain.

Pulling free of the now writhing vampire, Dane made a B-line for his mother as I worked myself the rest of the way free—with the help of Lupei. Yeah, Lupei! Dracula was distracted and I think that gave Lupei a momentary burst of total freedom, maybe for the first time in years.

I glanced back at Dracula as Lupei, muttering and jerking like he was in some sort of seizure, untied me. The vampire's face was bubbling like boiling water. And he was cradling his stomach like someone about to vomit up a bad batch of sushi. He stumbled to the floor, a gray foamy substance spilling from his lips. Lupei pulled me to my feet, muttering a stream of apologies and urging me to flee before it was too late.

Dane had freed Mrs. M and Lupei and I had just untied Anica when Dracula shouted, "No! I demand your loyalty!"

Lupei went rigid. His eyes went wide. By this point, Dracula was on the floor, globs of skin dripping from his face like pancake batter from a spatula. He was convulsing. But he'd reacquired control of Lupei. And Peter too—if he'd ever lost it. To be honest, I'd almost forgotten about Peter. He'd just been standing there through all of this. Just kind of blank like a department store mannequin. Like maybe his brain had been put on pause when Dracula was attacked.

I recognized the look in Lupei's eyes as he turned toward me. That, Drac-in-the-head look. Fortunately, I was quick enough to pull away from him, grab one of the fallen chairs, and smack him across the face with it just as he turned to attack me. I felt bad about it. I mean, I don't think any of this is really his fault. But, you know, survival instinct and all that.

Lupei tumbled to his right and I turned just in time to see Dracula slowly crawling toward me, blood spilling from his now malformed lips, gurgling hacks rumbling in his chest. Dane was fighting Peter, who was obviously under Dracula's control. But the guy didn't seem to be fighting too hard. I think he was probably trying to fight off the wavering influence of the dying vampire. He was doing that head shaky thing that Lupei does.

"A little help here," said Dane. "Grab some rope. We need to bind this bastard." He then landed a pretty fierce right hook to Peter's chin. And then another and another. Peter had killed his dad. I think Dane would have pummeled the guy to death if I hadn't shouted at him, bringing him back to reality.

Mrs. M and I both grabbed some of the fallen ropes. We tied Peter's hands behind his back while Dane held him more or less in place. Peter's face was bloody. So were Dane's knuckles. Anica seemed like she was pretty much back with us and was on her feet, though she had a bad case of the wobbles.

I thought about finding a weapon, maybe breaking one of the chairs and using a broken—hopefully jagged—leg as a stake to spike the vampire, but when I looked toward Dracula I knew just how stupid that idea was. He was a wounded beast, rolling around the floor in pain, but slashing this way and that, growling, gnashing his fangs. He was in a bad way but there was no chance we were getting anywhere near the guy without losing a limb or two.

Dane ran to the nearest window and pulled the curtains free. He then produced a lighter from his pocket and tried to light the curtain. The flame didn't take at first. It just kind of spread out across the fabric, but did nothing. But after a minute or so I saw the first wisps of smoke and then the beginnings of legitimate flames. Dane tossed the curtain toward Dracula. It fell a little short, but the fire was already growing. If the carpet caught and maybe some of the furnishings, who knew, maybe the whole place would burn. And with it, the vampire. High hopes, yeah, but a girl's got to have her dreams.

What I really wanted was to rescue Lupei, but Dracula had inched over to the man. The last thing I saw as Dane grabbed my arm and pulled me toward the door was Dracula burying his fangs in Lupei's neck. I'm guessing he needed new blood to help fight off the poison in his system. This vampire was not willing to concede.

Dane shouted. He'd managed to open the door. I don't know if it had been unlocked, if he'd forced it, or what. My attention had been on Dracula. But as quick as that we were outside, running, Dane harshly pulling Peter along, Mrs. M and Anica side by side, arms about each other. I could see flames rising from within as we moved past the impaled form of Anica's father. The poor girl screamed like I've never heard anyone scream before. But Mrs. M whispered to her as she guided her forward. I don't know what she said to the girl—or what could possibly help—but Anica moved forward, though her shrieks continued to echo off of the castle's stone walls.

We made our way down a sloping ridge, weaving through trees and brush. The moon was only a sliver and there was little natural light to illuminate our way. Not fun. I think every one of us tripped at least once. Peter—who stumbled at least three times—was still somewhere in the fuzzy la-la land between Dracula's control and true consciousness. He wasn't fighting against us, but he wasn't exactly what I'd call engaged either. Just kind of a dumb blank look.

We fled into the trees, Mrs. Mulligan still trying to quiet Anica. I remember thinking that the woman was in the midst of her own grief and here she was attempting to comfort another. She's a strong woman. Or, maybe it was just that she knew Anica would draw attention. Or maybe it was a way of keeping her mind off of her own loss. I don't know, but I was impressed by the lady, that's for sure.

Soon we were fully into the woods, the castle falling further and further into the distance behind us. But still I kept looking over my shoulder, expecting to see Dracula on my heals. By all logic he was dead—or at least near-dead—but I didn't trust it. That monster was like a cat, nine lives or more. At least that's the way it seemed.

We continued deeper into the forest, no breaks, no hesitation, though we did eventually slow into a more sustainable pace. Something had been bugging me since our encounter with Dracula. Something that really nettled me to the point where I wanted to scream, and so I moved to alongside Dane. "Hey," I said.

Not bothering to look toward me, he said. "What's up?"

"You had the vial. The blood from the ancient vampire goddess."

"Yeah. And?"

"How'd you get it?"

A frown. Still no eye contact. "What do you mean?"

"Serghei had it. The Romani gave it to him. How'd you get it?"

He tossed me one of those dismissive shrugs that says, I-really-don't-want-to-go-there. "From Serghei."

"Voluntarily?"

"And what's that supposed to mean?"

I glanced back over my shoulder to make sure Anica wasn't within ear-shot and then whispered, "If Serghei had the vial when Lavinia attacked him he might be alive right now."

"You don't know that."

"For sure? Of course not. But he'd have stood the same chance you did in there. He might still be alive for Anica."

"That's a big assumption, Kiddo."

"I'm not a kiddo and it's not too much of a stretch. You stole his only weapon and left him at the mercy of the vampires."

He continued walking for maybe thirty seconds before responding. "Survival of the fittest. I do what I have to do to survive."

"And everyone else be damned, is that the idea?"

"That's not the goal. But, unfortunately, sometimes, yeah, that's how things turn out." He paused, finally turning to look at me. "I'm not happy about it, okay? I didn't want it to go down that way. How could I know Serghei would be the first target? I've got Van Helsing blood creeping through my veins. I was sure I'd be at the top of the hit list."

I was about to tell him that this was no excuse, that he had no right to steal the vial, that at the very least he should have gone to Serghei with his concerns and asked if he could have the blood. I called him a lowlife, saying that he must have been a huge disappointment to his parents. But that was as far as it had gone when the wolves attacked and I didn't have a chance to say anything other than, "Look out!"

I think there were six of them. But it was dark and everything went from calm to outright chaos in less than a second. A large gray wolf pounced on Dane, locking its jaws on his left forearm. Blood splattered across the animal's face and Dane let out a howl to rival one from the wolf itself. I heard screams from behind as Mrs. M and Peter were attacked. Anica stood off to the side, apparently paralyzed by fear. She did nothing to defend herself or her companions. Who can say what she was thinking in those moments? Dane fell to the ground fighting against the wolf as I grabbed a fallen tree branch from the ground and smacked an oncoming wolf in the face with a golf-like swing.

There was another wolf coming at me from the left and I swung the branch back and forth, attempting to fend it off. But then the first wolf that I'd hit charged me again. I was swinging my branch back and forth, trying to keep two wolves at bay, but I knew this would buy me seconds at best. I could see Mrs. M throwing stones at one that was pouncing on Peter—whose arms were still tied behind his back. And Dane was still rolling around the ground smacking at the one that was locked on his arm. And then the first gunshot echoed through the woods. And then another. And another.

It was the Romani. The ones that had given the vial to Serghei, the ones that had helped us get to the castle. They took out every one of the wolves with well-placed shots. Even though we were all in motion, battling for our lives, in close proximity to the blood-crazed beasts, not one of us was hit and not one of the wolves survived. They saved us.

We'd escaped Dracula's castle alive.

Looking back on it later, I think that normal wolves would have fled after the first gunshot. Or, at the very least, turned to face the sound. But these continued with the attack, not even acknowledging the weapons, until one by one they fell, each struck by bullets. And because of this, I'm sure those weren't ordinary wolves. They were under Dracula's control. Not one wolf attacked Anica—Dracula's "love." But they went nuclear on the Van Helsing team. And so I'm sure, even though his castle was gutted with flames, even though I've been assured that no one could have lived through that blaze, I know that Dracula still lives. And some day, some time, he'll come looking for a reckoning.

From the personal blog of Peter Van Helsing
April 10, 2015

Next week will be a year. That's insane. A year. They say time flies. And it does. But then it also creeps. That doesn't make sense, but it's the truth. In some ways it feels like those insane horrible events, those poor decisions, those lives lost, it feels like yesterday. But then it also feels like a scene from some long-ago crazy other lifetime.

Did it even happen? Was I truly stupid enough to track Dracula? Apparently I was. Idiot! I was an idiot. I was trying to prove something, wasn't I? I thought I could be the hero father. Impress my kids. I had Van Helsing blood. Famous vampire hunters. I would slay the vampire legend myself. Well, a swelled ego is not much more than an excuse for bad behavior. And it lead to disaster. People died trying to rescues me. People that I'd never even met. They risked their lives for me and two of them lost—one at my own hand.

In case you haven't figured it out, that's a heavy burden. I considered becoming an alcoholic. I mean, that would be the cliché, right? Hey, the guy ruined a bunch of lives, was responsible for some deaths. Now let's watch him spiral into alcoholic abuse and addiction.

But, no. That's not me.

Oh, I'm not saying that I'm that strong. No, not at all. What I mean is that I didn't avoid that slippery slope out of some great will power. No. I wallowed plenty. I just had a different take on self-destruction. You see, after returning to the States I don't think I know exactly what I did. I was free of Dracula's influence, I'm sure of that. I mean, if he still lives, and who am I kidding, of course he does, then an ocean separates us. His mental control is strong, but there are limitations. But, just because I was free of his crazy mental rape doesn't mean I was whole.

I mean, guilt is the real monster, right? And shock. And, let's not forget trauma. Post Traumatic Stress Syndrome, that's a thing. PTSD. Cool lingo that essentially means, you're screwed. So, what I'm saying is I spent about four months just sitting on a pier staring out over Lake Michigan. I didn't O.D. I didn't jump off a bridge or walk into a crowd with an Uzi. I just gazed at the waves. I might've been thinking about something. That would make sense. A guy sits in the same spot day after day just staring out at the undulating water, he's got to have something sloshing around the cranium. Oh look, it's raining. The guy's still there. Wow, beautiful girls in bikinis. Not even a glance. Zero interest. Oh hey, is that a tornado warning? Yeah, the moron's still sitting there. He must be contemplating reality or figuring out the solution to global warming or conceptualizing the next major technological leap, like maybe, oh, I don't know, computer generated telekinesis. Something monumental. Something beyond the scope of normalcy.

Nah.

Mostly I was pretty much thinking about nothing.

Yeah. Nothing. Nada. Just a blank slate. Dull inside. Emotionally dead. Disconnected. Lethargic. If I'd learned, in that time, that I had a terminal illness and had less than a month to live, I don't think I would have taken action. I'd probably have just shrugged and continued staring at the waves and tapping on my bongos. In retrospect, maybe alcoholism would have been the better way to go. At least then I'd have an excuse for dropping out of life.

But, I did come back. I can't say why. I can't even say what incited the change. I was just sitting there one day and all of a sudden the lethargy just dripped away. That probably sounds strange. Drip away, right? But it's the best description I have. It was like the weight on my limbs just dribbled to the ground and I was ready to move.

But move on to what?

Now, there was a question.

I had energy. Where had that come from? I mean, Mr. Stupor on valium with a hangover, that's what I'd been like. And then—boom! —bouncy as a puppy, only no puddles on the living room carpet. It was as if all of the clouds muddling my brain just burned away in the morning sun. I don't attribute this to anything specific. There was no spiritual epiphany. I didn't get onto some California all-veggie energizer bunny diet. I did nothing at all to change it.

Well, I did hear a song that morning. It stuck in my head the way they do. "I Want You to Want Me" by Cheap Trick. An old song—before my time. But everybody knows that tune. Doesn't matter if you were born after its release. Catchy. Bouncy. It kept rebounding around my head. Maybe that was all it took. Four chords, a solid beat, and a catchy hook. Or maybe it was just time. Maybe I was just a little too tired of being tired.

But here I was, brain engaged. What next? That was the nuclear question. If you think about it, it was probably the only question. I'd walked away from my life in order to chase a vampire. God, that sounds stupid. The question, the real honest to God question is, what kind of guy does that? Man, I have kids to think about. Yeah. I'd lost custody, but did I think that defeating Dracula was going to be my ticket to father of the year? That's insane. Probably, and this was not a conscious thing, but probably I was going off to die. Killed at the hands of the most famous vampire ever. A big finale. My kids would be proud of me and I'd never have to face their disappointment again. Any disappointment. No more failures. No more almost but not quite.

That was probably it. Somewhere deep inside, that was the goal.

So again, the question tossing around my freshly reengaged brain was, now what?

My kids, of course. See my kids. Cool. Now that my emotions had been switched back to the "on" mode. It was like being slammed in the gut by a baseball bat, that moment when I realized how much I missed them. Pricilla was heading into her senior year in high school, Steve, his freshman year. These were significant times in their lives and I was missing them. I pictured their faces: Steve, his dark hair splashed across his forehead, nearly covering his left eye, his broad lips twisted into a grin. I wanted to see him pursue his art. He was good, especially with pastels. I mean there's awesome talent there. And Pricilla. Oh, my little princess, growing up so fast. I wanted to be there to protect her from every boy ever born. I can't express how much I wanted to hug her in that moment, to gaze into her rich brown eyes. She played soccer and was good at it. Maybe scholarship good. Not Division One, but maybe a shot at Two or almost definitely Three. She'd never be an Olympian, but she could have had good shot at getting a free education out of the game. Not bad for a kid with a screwed up head case of a dad and a spiteful mom. Oh, my little girl. The tears of loss flooded over my cheeks. Immediately, still sitting on that beach, fresh from the Wham!-you're-human-again moment, I called Vanessa, my bitter, vindictive, Satan-in-yoga-pants ex-wife.

Go figure, the call didn't go well. Apparently, in my absence, both abroad and since my return, Vanessa had been working with her lawyer to carve me completely out of the children's lives. She charged me with abandonment. She used the fact that I withdrew all of my money from both savings and retirement to run off hunting vampires and hadn't so much as called to check on the kids since my return as cause. She even used my In Search of Dracula YouTube videos as evidence.

No surprise the judge agreed with her.

I argued my case, of course. I pleaded, hoping to connect with her humanity, some sense of compassion or fondness for what we'd once shared. But she just hung up every time I called. I hired a cheap attorney because, Vanessa was right about one thing, I had blown through nearly all of my money on that insane expedition and hadn't made any new money since returning. She wasn't going to budge and had all of the facts on her side. I had abandoned them. I hadn't stayed to fight, to be a part of their lives after Vanessa left me. I'd spun out and now she couldn't see, didn't want to see, that I'd landed back at ground zero, that I was whole again and ready and anxious to resume my role in my kid's lives.

That all happened back in August. Or I should say it started in August, when I came out of the haze. It's now April. Yeah, eight months if you're into counting, and I'm still fighting for some small chance to see my kids every once in a while.

It sucks.

What else have I done since then?

I guess the most noteworthy thing is that I help my Aunt Lizzy.

This might seem weird. And it is. But she's family. Think about it. I'd never known her before my crazy misadventure and yet she raced across the world to save me.

And then I killed her husband.

Oh, I don't blame myself for that. Not in any rational way. Don't get the wrong impression. I'm no sociopath with no empathy or sense of guilt. I feel guilt. Plenty of guilt for most of what happened during that time. But the killing of Uncle Conner? Yeah, I have guilt that I'd put him in that position, but not guilt for being the instrument of his death. That's an odd distinction, I know. But I was under Dracula's control at the time and have almost zero recollection of anything that happened. But, Conner wouldn't have been there if not for me. I'd set that Dracula ball in motion. That was my doing. That was my sin. That he was there at all.

Lizzy was a strong woman prior to Wallachia. Even though she was advanced in years, she was active and clear minded. She and Conner, though officially retired, had still kept a hand in the operation of the family business. She was fit and strong willed and most people took her as being nearly two decades younger than her actual age.

Not now.

The Lizzy I know walks through her days in a haze. She talks about Conner, always about Conner. She's accepted me into her life, but there's disdain when she looks at me. I don't think she'll ever get over the fact that I'm the one who took Conner from her. And yeah, who could blame her? But here I am, offering hot cocoa and cleaning up her spills. On most days I want to walk away. She doesn't want me, the constant reminder of what she's lost, hovering over her. But I already abandoned one family. I'm not going to do the same to another. I put her in this position and I'm going to see her through it. I know there's still strength in her. I see hints of the real Lizzy. Little glimpses of that determination and drive. There and then gone. But one of these days she'll snap out of it. I'm sure of it.

Oh, and she gave me a job. Kind of. Put me on the payroll of the family business. I.T. Technical support. Computer geek stuff. It's my thing, so it fits. There's not much call for my skills. I almost never have to go in. But Lizzy says that I should have been part of the business for years, that as Stephen's son I'm part owner and so this isn't a charity, but just a way of giving me what is already mine. I take this as a good sign. I'm not saying it means she's forgiven me. But it's probably an indication that she knows that

I never meant for any of this to happen. And it's Lizzy being proactive. One of those little hints that the old Lizzy is still in there somewhere.

I think she might have also done it, in part, because her own son, Dane, is… God, what can I say about Dane? We hear from him occasionally, but it's usually when he wants money. It seems he's always in a different state and he always has some crazy plan that's going to make him a millionaire. I don't know Dane well. Just that short time in Wallachia and then a handful of short encounters since, but he seems a little sketchy. Maybe living on the fringes of the law. Not my business, I guess. But it's almost as if he has a grudge against his mother, like maybe he blames her for his dad's death. She was the Van Helsing—the vampire hunter. His dad had been drawn in by her and therefore it was her fault that he'd died. I don't know for sure that this is the thinking, but it's what I've gathered from snatches of conversation I've overheard. Also, he considers the family business a joke—except when he wants his share of the profits.

Oh! And speaking of the business, the detective agency branch, not the dry cleaning side, Kerri Rivera heads that up now. I think she impressed my Aunt Lizzy while in Wallachia. From what I understand, she held her own pretty well over there despite being little more than a desk clerk for the firm. Good for her. I like Kerri. She's not family, but none of us blood Van Helsings have earned the position.

But, now I have to wonder, what next? I feel we're all in some kind of crazy holding pattern. Just waiting for something to break. For something to jolt us out of our complacency. And I don't think I'm cool with what form that might take.

From the journal of Kerri Rivera
May 02, 2015

So, I'm entering this in my personal journal, not the official Van Helsing Investigations journal because this isn't an official case. It's just my own private thing. Kind of a "looking into" more than an investigation.

There are two things I'm recording here—kind of related, but separate nonetheless. Neither are things I want Mrs. Mulligan stumbling across right now. The first has to do with Dane. Yeah, I've investigated him, okay? Not investigated—officially, or even in any massively thorough go-for-the-jugular way. Just, keeping an eye on him—kind of. From a distance. I mean the guy's part owner of Van Helsing Investigations, I don't think I want a traceable record of me looking into his shadyesque activities. And he can be shady. Not full on criminal-for-hire stuff. He's not with the mob. He doesn't run drugs or act as a hired gun. Not that I know of. God! That'd suck!

No. He just… schemes. Yeah. He has schemes. Make-a-buck-quick kind of stuff. Business dealings that sketch the shady side—apparently. Maybe acquiring merchandise from not-so reputable sources, maybe getting loans from non-traditional sources. Sketchy, but not flagrant.

It's all weird. He delves into something, starts making deals with people, makes huge promises to move this or that product, that he can get some great distribution deal for TVs, or furniture—beard trimmers. Whatever happens to lands in his lap. And he'll start making calls, and collecting money and then—Blamo! —he drops that and races off to something else. It's like he wants to be some sort of hot shot black market type but doesn't really want to land too firmly on that side of the fence. Like maybe it fuels his ego but not his conscience. I don't think Dane's a bad guy. I think what he's really trying to do is to not be a Van Helsing. Too much legacy. Too much responsibility. Too many stakes and crosses. So he's kind of trying to find something that's completely opposite of that.

I've talked with him a few times, offered to get him involved with the firm. I mean, I'm the one running this place now and I'm not even family. So, you know, trying to show the guy some courtesy. No go. Not a chance. In his words, "Leave me the hell out of it."

I've encouraged him to check in on his mom more frequently. The response: "None of your damned business."

We've had this kind of quasi-antagonistic, quasi-just-kidding banter going on for a while now. I've cautioned him about some of his squirrely business dealings. Again, "None of your damned business."

And that's why I was a little freaked out by a call I got from Dane this morning.

It went something like this:

"Hey, kid." (BTW, I'm older than Dane by a full decade.)

"Dane?"

"Not the tooth fairy."

"Oh, hi. Back in Chicago? Last I knew you were in New Jersey. Some big waffle iron scheme, right?"

"You've got to stop snooping into my business, kid. And it was restaurant supply equipment—all legal. I got a great deal on the stuff from a connection and unloaded it for a killing."

"Wonderful. You're a real player. I'm not a kid."

"Right. So, you talked with my mom at all this week? She okay?"

Well, that was weird. He never asks about her, not to me at least. "I talked with her, I don't know, a few days ago. Maybe last week like Friday or something."

"Was she okay? How did she sound?"

"Fine. Normal. I mean, normal for how she is now, not for how she was, you know, before your dad died. Why? What's wrong?"

"She didn't say anything, did she?"

Now I was starting to think something was up. "About what?"

He paused. One of those how-do-I-say-this-without-really-saying-it pauses. "Just anything strange."

"A little more specific please."

Double that pause this time. And then, "Vampires."

Okay. That's the taboo subject. Dane likes to pretend like none of the events over in Wallachia ever occurred. "What's up, Dane? Get off the dance floor."

"Huh?"

"Stop dancing around it."

"Oh. Got it. So, I saw one. Here. Chicago." He practically whispered it. Like maybe he didn't want anyone to hear him.

"A vampire? You saw a vampire? Are you sure?"

"Yeah. A vampire. And yes, I'm sure. I know the look. A little too well, if you ask me."

"But, there are no vampires in Chicago. Not in, I don't know, decades. Not since Dracula left."

"Yeah. Exactly. So, what's happening, Kerri? You're supposed to be the girl in the know."

But I didn't know. This was the first I'd heard of any of this. I told Dane I'd check into it. And then he hung up. Just hung up. No, "Thanks, kid," no, "Okay, I'll get back to you," just click. And so then I contacted Peter, Mrs. M, and Anica, each separately.

And now I'm wondering just what we're up against.

Transcript of a text conversation between Kerri Rivera, Peter Van Helsing, and Anica Ardelean May 02, 2015

Kerri: Hey, guys. Had a weird conversation with Dane this morning. Anything strange going on in your necks of the woods?

Peter: Weird conversation with Dane? And this is different how?

Anica: I'm not sure I understand what you mean by weird. Are you referring to something humorous?

Kerri: Vampire weird.

Anica: Oh dear. Here? In The United States?

Kerri: Chicago.

Peter: Nah! Dane's pulling one of his idiotic stunts. I bet there's a get rich quick scam in this.

Kerri: I don't think so. He sounded kind of freaked.

Anica: Dracula? Is it Dracula? Please tell me it's not Dracula.

Kerri: I don't think so, Anica.

Peter: Okay. If this is real, it's got to be connected to Dracula.

Kerri: He saw a vampire. It wasn't Dracula. I've been searching through police reports all day. Haven't found anything that looks vampy yet, but I'm believing Dane on this one.

Peter: I'm not saying Dane's fang fiend was Dracula. But Drac made all of the vampires in Chicago. Lizzy and Conner killed them all after he escaped back to Europe. If there are vampires in Chicago again, you can be damn sure it means Dracula's back.

Anica: Oh my God. I must leave. I can't. No. I can't go through that again. I can't.

Kerri: Anica, don't panic. We really don't know anything yet. Have either of you seen anything weird? Peter, what about Mrs. M? Is she alright? Has she mentioned anything?

Anica: I haven't seen anything, but this is horrible, horrible news.

Peter: Nothing. Saw Lizzy this morning. She was the same as always. Lethargic and uninterested in anything more challenging than The Price is Right.

Kerri: Okay. So, we have to assume Dracula's back. But he hasn't made a move yet—other than to make at least one new vamp. So, don't throw the panic switch. Peter, can you get to Mrs. M and stay there? Anica, you shouldn't be alone after dark. Also, its garlic time. Get garlic oil, get crosses, carry a knife or a gun—or both. Game on, kids. If Dracula's here we need to be ready.

Peter: I'm not exactly stoked about facing Drac again. We need a plan.

Kerri: Yep. Agreed. Any thoughts on that?

Peter: Catch the next plane to Tahiti.

Anica: I'm scared.

Kerri: Okay. It's already dusk, not a good time to be moving around. Let's think about our options and stay in contact. Anica, do you have someplace close that you can stay for the night? Someplace where you're not alone?

Anica: No. Not that I can think of.

Kerri: Okay, I'll come to you. With rush hour traffic I can be there in about an hour and a half. I'll bring the garlic and crosses. Stay locked in. Don't answer your door. Peter, grab supplies and get to Mrs. M.

Peter: I'm on it.

Anica: Please hurry.

Transcript of email sent to Lenuta Ardelean from Anica Ardelean May 02, 2015

Mama, I so wish you were here. I know you did not want me to come all the way to The United States, especially right after what happened to Papa, but I felt it was the only way to put enough distance between Dracula and myself to ensure that I was beyond his influence. But, Mama. Now it seems he may have found me. All of these thousands of miles away, and he may be upon my very doorstep.

I don't know what to do. It seems a vampire has been seen in Chicago. Not Dracula, but still there is concern. My friend Kerri is on her way to me and I am going to suggest that we both flee to another city, at least until we know for sure that we are safe from this demon.

I hate so much to do this. I have found a job that I like very much. And, Mama, there is a young man. His name is Paul and we have begun dating. He is not here right now, but is out of town visiting family. I wish so much I could stay instead of running like a rabbit from a fox, but it seems I must.

Is this my life now, Mama? Am I always to be running, to be hiding? Can I never be free of this horrible monster? Can I never have a normal life?

I'm sorry. I'm probably frightening you terribly. I'm sure I am overreacting. I'll be fine. The sighted vampire was not Dracula and was not in my area of this vast metropolis. I have good friends here. Brave friends. We will see this through.

And, Mama. I know you claim that you're happy staying in the village with Aunt Lerae, but please reconsider my offer to come and live with me. I miss you so and I believe you would find Chicago fascinating.

I love you so dearly. Please don't worry. I'm just being silly. All is fine here.

Love, Anica.

From the journal of Vlad Dracula
May 02, 2015

She was alone. My beautiful Anica. Such a precious sparrow. Her rich dark hair spilled over her shoulders as she paced one way and then another before the window, a phone clutched in her palm as her thumbs danced across the tiny screen. Her skin was rich in tone, not so perfectly white as upon our past encounters, but with a touch of the sun, a subtle darkening. Not much more than a dash of pigment. And yet it added a warmth to her appearance, a flare, perhaps a suggestion of underlying fervor or passion. I sat on the roof of the building adjacent her apartment, gazing at her as might a lustful adolescent. How I longed for her in that moment. Simply to be in her presence, to hear her laugh, to see her eyes gleam with joy as she said my name.

And strangely, my mind flitted away from Anica and to thoughts of Lavinia. Of those early years together. For her eyes did light when they fell upon me. Her blood did boil with passion and greed for my touch. We truly were as youths locked in that eternal moment of endless desire. Never did she reject me. Not once did she cast her eyes in search of another mate. She had welcomed my gift of the eternal midnight, and in doing so, had given herself to me completely.

A memory pushed its way into my thoughts, a memory of a night some two centuries past. We had tired of our secluded existence situated on the fringes of civilization. We knew that for those such as us this was an ideal locale settled within easy reach of our prey, the fearful and superstitious peasants, and away from curious eyes of the troublesome educated class who tended to question and confront rather than to flee. But we had determined that occasional excursions into urban centers would be healthy diversions. And so we left the castle in the care of my two lesser brides and took up temporary residence in a rented estate in Bucharest.

On the night in question we had spotted a young couple, honeymooners as we soon learned. They were giddy in their love for one another and oblivious to any danger the world might thrust upon them. As is the case with so many youths, they believed themselves to be invincible. For they were young and in love. Who would dare intrude on such a magical time? Lavinia found them outrageously entertaining and mimicked their proclamations of love and their awkward and tentative public groping. So anxious, but yet so concerned about being seen. What possibly would people think if they learned that young couples felt physical desire? Such a scandal it would be. Humans can truly be ridiculous in so many ways with their moral taboos and tenuous proclamations of virtue. Why is it they feel they must deny their very nature, the drives that shape them, the passions that grant them vision and courage, if not a hefty dose of stupidity from time to time? I tried to remember if I had behaved such during my living years and must suppose that I had. To a point, at least. I was, after all, pledged to the sacred church. But I was also of royal blood which carried with it a certain leniency toward standards imposed rigidly upon the working class.

I laughed at Lavinia's often lewd and raucous jokes as we followed far behind the entwined couple. It was late into the evening and the streets were becoming less populated. But a vampire's senses are much more acute than those of the human. We could easily see and hear all that happened without coming close enough to ever be noticed. We could even smell the hormones racing through their veins. And hear the pulsing hearts filled with delectable blood. Lavinia kissed me full on the mouth, nipping at my lower lip and then sipping at the small trickle of blood produced by her bite. "We must have them," she said. "And then we must partake of one another." She licked my cheek and then nibbled at my ear. Ah, Lavinia. Always the wildcat. Never content to simply exist. Like me, she was driven to experience every moment to its fullest.

The couple wove through the streets, sneaking kisses and stealing the occasional forbidden squeeze, stumbling almost drunkenly as they made their way to their tiny apartment.

"Oh," cried Lavinia with a wink as they entered the two story dwelling. "Whatever could they possibly have planned?"

There was no question of their intent. The two were so filled with lust they had nearly copulated on the street. There was little doubt what was to follow.

Allowing them nearly ten minutes to be fully distracted, we then climbed the narrow staircase to the tiny apartment. Lavinia approached the door and called, "Please, dear one. Come to me. I must see you at once." We could hear the rustle of fabric and murmured questions. But Lavinia shared some of my more advanced attributes and was able touch the young male's mind. The control was not as firm as it would have been had he tasted her blood, but she was strong in the gift and the lad was thoroughly enraptured in the physical, his mind nearly disengaged. He was ripe for the taking. "Come, dear boy," she said. "For more fleshly pleasure awaits than you could ever imagine. You need simply open the door."

I could hear the girl protesting, but the young man quieted her with a sharp rebuke and moved toward the entrance.

"Yes, my young friend. Come to me. Meet your destiny." Lavinia smiled and licked her lips in anticipation.

I could sense the boy's conflict. He was faithful to his mate and wanted only to return to their shared bed, but Lavinia had infused an irrational desire for her within him. And so when he opened the door he already had an image of her loveliness upon his brain. He wore only his trousers, the shirt and footwear had been discarded. His expression was a mixture of confusion and desire, but when Lavinia said, "My darling, you will allow us to enter," he simply nodded and stepped aside, never taking his eyes from Lavinia's hypnotic gaze.

The woman, though, was not enthralled and shouted at us and at her man. Lavinia, always the antagonist, turned, kissing the boy passionately, nearly smothering him with her full moist lips.

The outraged woman shouted from the bed where she was covered only by a sheet she pressed against her bosom. I grinned and ordered her to cease with her prattle. I felt only the mildest mental struggle before she calmed and sat passively awaiting my next command. "Woman," I said. "Go to your kitchen. Fetch a knife." Her eyes widened only slightly, her jaw twitched only just, as if she thought to protest, and then, silently, she slid from the bed and passed before me, now unconcerned with her nakedness. Moments later she stood before me holding a long curved blade. "Very good," I said. "My companion is quite thirsty, slice your lover's wrist so that she might drink." There was that mental push I had anticipated. The woman sought to resist my will, but she was simply not up to the task.

The young man was still enthralled by Lavinia and, at her instruction, offered his wrist to his bride. There was a moment, only a moment, where their eyes met and I thought there might be some slight resistance. But there was none. Quickly, with the efficiency of one accustomed to slaying chickens for the evening meal, the woman sliced through her mate's flesh sending a fountain of blood pulsing onto her naked chest.

Smiling, Lavinia stepped forward to partake of the feast as the woman stood silently by, watching her beloved's life blood sucked into Lavinia's gorgeous lips. I could feel her horror, her revulsion, but pushed her, just enough to make her remain still. Eventually, the boy's knees buckled and Lavinia lowered him gently to the floor. Her face was red with blood and her grin was broad. The boy twitched and gasped, still alive, but only just.

Lavinia came to me then, her eyes sparkling with that glistening hint of red. "Hungry?" she asked. Grinning, I released the girl from my control, allowing her to fall screaming and weeping before her dying lover. Lavinia offered her neck to me and I greedily partook of her precious blood which was intermingled with that of the still dying lad. She unfastened my shirt and tugging slightly, slipped it away to fall to the floor. It was to be a magnificent night.

And there I sat, centuries later, on a rooftop, staring across at the agitated Anica. And I wondered, could I ever share such a moment with her? And did I desire to do so? Lavinia, I believe, like me, was born to walk the eternal midnight. If I had not come to her on that eve, offering her this dreadful gift, she would likely have lived an unfulfilled life, knowing there was something more for her but never understanding what that might be. But Anica is different. Initially, I did not intend to offer her the gift, at least not until she had accepted its value. But she has rejected me repeatedly and so I find that I must lead her into the eternal midnight. But I ponder, will she accept this new life I offer? Certainly not at the onset. No. She despises all that I represent and, in her humanity, will never accept me as anything but a fiend. But, should I grant her my blood, once the gift has taken hold, once she has experienced the joy of draining a person's life, drop by drop from their veins, of sharing their horrified mind as the realization that death is upon them, will she then embrace the gift? For it is a gift. An offer of immortality, of strength and vigor beyond human comprehension. Will she accept this precious thing that I offer? I suppose only time will tell.

Transcript of text conversation between Kerri Rivera and Peter Van Helsing May 02, 2015

Kerri: I'm at Anica's apartment. She's not here. Have you heard from her?

Peter: No. Are there any signs of a break-in or a struggle?

Kerri: No.

Peter: I'm assuming you haven't been able to reach her.

Kerri: Bingo. She's in the wind. How's Mrs. M?

Peter: Actually, pretty with it. The thought of Dracula being here shocked her out of her stupor. She's racing all over the place assembling her vampire fighting gear, preparing for battle. It's like she's an entirely different person. But Kerri, you need to get out of there. If Anica's been taken, Dracula may still be close, maybe even watching you now. You shouldn't be alone.

Kerri: I'll meet you at Mrs. M's. But first I'll call Anica's boyfriend and some of her work associates to see if she's made contact.

Peter: Do that en route, Kerri. Just get out of there.

Kerri: Hold on. I think someone might…

From the Files of Van Helsing Investigations
June 21, 2015

NO CASE NUMBER
NOTES FROM JUNE 21, 2015
AS RECORDED BY LIZZY VAN HELSING-MULLIGAN

Anica and Kerri have been missing for nearly two months now. Peter, Dane, and I have followed every potential lead, every potential vampire siting, every seemingly mysterious death. We've scoured recent real estate purchases in the Chicagoland area hoping to find a name connected to Dracula. You see, in the past, he has been known to use pseudonyms based on the names of former opponents. For instance, once, many years ago, he purchased an estate under the name of Jonathan Harker, a man he'd fought in the 1890s. But at that time he'd wanted us to find him. He'd laid a trap. No such luck this time. We've found nothing.

There's tension between us. Not just because of our failure to locate our missing friends, but our little group is dysfunctional at its core. Peter killed my husband. Yes, he was under Dracula's spell at the time, and yes, he essentially acted as my nurse during the dark lethargic haze of my grief, but it was his doing. Everything was Peter's doing, all of it. The fact that he was under Dracula's influence when he stabbed Conner doesn't mitigate the fact that it was Peter's foolhardy adventure that brought us to Europe—to Dracula—in the first place. No matter what he does in an attempt to make up for it, the fact is, I lost my husband and Anica lost her father because of Peter's smallminded selfishness.

And Dane. Yes, Dane is my son, and of course I love him. But he's chosen to live his life separated from us, often, I believe, making choices specifically on the criteria that it would be the opposite of what Conner or I would have wanted. Dane is a rebel for rebel's sake. It could be excused in an adolescent, not so for a man in his forties. Add to this that Dane considers Peter a useless loser and Peter thinks Dane a scoundrel and it's no wonder we've been an ineffective team. I'm not sure that we would have ever found a single clue to Dracula's location if not for Lavinia.

She was there this past evening. At my home. Simply standing on the front lawn and calling to us through the open window, asking permission to enter. Peter recognized her immediately. After a moment's hesitation, he raced through the doorway and nearly stumbled onto the lawn before her.

Peter was unarmed. I don't know if this was intentional or if it simply didn't occur to him that a weapon might be useful. I grabbed my always-present crossbow, the same one owned by my brother Stephen all those years ago and then by Conner until his death, and moved toward the doorway.

"Whoa, whoa, whoa," said Dane. "What do you think you're doing?"

"It seems pretty obvious to me."

"That's a vampire out there."

I rolled my eyes and said, "Vampires? No don't think I've ever encountered those before," as I marched through the doorway with far less confidence than what I portrayed. Dane cursed and then snatched a revolver from the end table and followed.

"You're supposed to be dead," said Peter to Lavinia as I moved to beside him.

The vampire smiled. Confident, unconcerned with our weapons. She wore modern attire, a loose-fitting cotton blouse (peach), stone-washed blue jeans, fashionable laced boots that stopped mid shin. Not very vampire-looking at all. More of a girl-on-the-way-to-the-mall look than an I'm-gonna-suck-you-dry motif. To most people she would appear as nothing more than an attractive young woman out for an evening stroll. "I do not die easily," said Lavinia. "I was made by Dracula himself and have feasted on his blood for centuries. I share his talents—as well as his tenacity when it comes to survival."

"Yeah, about that," said Peter. "Dracula left you outside where the sun could finish you off. That should have nuked you straight to hell."

She shrugged. "By my count, Dracula has perished three times since entering the eternal midnight. Yet, he still thrives."

"That's Dracula. He's had some crazy magic put in place to resurrect him."

A broad grin. "Yes he has." She offered nothing more, but obviously the implication was that Dracula was not the only one who had acquired mystical fortifications.

Dane was beside me now, the revolver aimed at the smiling Lavinia. "Yeah, yeah," he said. "Not really interested in your chit-chat. You haven't attacked us, you made yourself obvious, so you obviously want something from us. Give me a reason why I shouldn't put a bullet through that putrid thing you call a heart." He tightened his grip on the pistol and offered what I'm certain he considered to be his best menacing expression. Most people are under the mistaken notion that guns are useless against vampires, that only wooden stakes, garlic, crosses, and the sun can kill one. Not so. Though vampires are much heartier than humans, they can be killed by many of the same means as us. True, the injury must be to the heart, but a bullet is as good as a stake. We Van Helsings tend to avoid guns mostly because vampires are so fast that attempting to strike them with gunfire is more likely to strike our companions than it is our targets. This has happened in the past and we've decided it best to go with seemingly more primitive—yet highly effective—weapons.

Lavinia appraised Dane, but then responded while gazing directly at me. "Elizabeth Van Helsing, I will address you as I feel you are the one most likely to deal with me in some reasonable fashion. I did not come here as a foe. Not on this occasion, at least."

"Then why are you here?" asked Dane.

Ignoring my son, Lavinia said, "As I'm sure you are aware, Dracula holds two of your companions."

"Yeah. That was pretty much our take on the situation," said Peter.

I said, "Are you telling me they're still alive?"

"Alive, yes. In his thrall? Yes, also."

"And why should we believe you?" asked Dane.

"As you have already stated, Dracula sought to have me slain simply as a means of regaining the favor of the mortal girl. He does not know that I live and your intervention would suit my objectives." Her lips quivered with fury as she spoke, a very human trait. This was a woman scorned, seeking revenge on a man she both loves and hates.

"Okay," said Peter. "And what crazy objectives are we talking?"

"The objective of every spurned woman throughout all of history. I desire him brought to ruin. I want him embarrassed and humbled."

"So, the purest of motives," said Dane.

I said, "I don't trust you."

She offered a throaty laugh. "And why would you? But here's the crux of it. You know that Dracula sought to take my life. You know that he has the two mortal girls. And you know that without the information I offer, you will likely never see your companions again."

"How do we know they're alive?" asked Dane.

"You don't. But I've come in good faith." She paused, her gaze meeting each of us. "I will give you the location of Dracula's residence. You will then deliberate throughout the night before finally deciding that you have no choice but to investigate."

She was right, of course. Lavinia gave us an address before disappearing into the shadows and we spent the entire night arguing amongst ourselves before finally determining that if we ever hoped to see Kerri and Anica again, there really was no other option.

God help us, we are once again going into Dracula's lair.

Written statement by Dane Van Helsing
June 25, 2015

I'm writing this only because my lawyer said I need to set the record straight. I.e., tell my side of the story. Not sure why it really matters because I don't expect many people to believe a word of it. I guess that's a little too bad, but not my problem. For the record, every word of this statement is the honest to God truth. So, either keep an open mind or stop reading right now because this isn't pretty and it's going to stretch your nice little world view into some twisted origami version of reality.

Not sure where to begin, but I think the others have recorded pretty much everything important up to that final night. So, God, I guess that's where I should start. The final night. That's what my attorney's concerned about anyway. That insane unbelievable night.

That vampire bitch Lavinia gave us an address. Dracula's lair, or so she claimed. I didn't believe her and even the small part of me that did believe didn't want to go charging into Dracula's digs. As far as I was concerned, Anica and Kerri were already lost. Not a happy thought, but realistic. What could we possibly hope to accomplish by putting ourselves in further danger? Dracula was obviously after Anica. He probably had her, had probably already turned her into a midnight freak. Bad news for her, but too late to do anything about it. I'm not saying I didn't feel any compassion for these girls, I'm just saying that in my mind it was already far too late to do them any good.

Lizzy and Peter saw things differently.

Of course.

For the record, Lizzy's my mom. But it's easier to just refer to her as Lizzy in this statement. It takes away any confusion about who I'm talking about to those people that don't know us.

So, there we were, all geared up with Lizzy's favorite vamp-stopping arsenal and ready to face-fang face again. Lizzy had the crossbow and her

Bowie knife. Peter and I both had three foot long blades—swords really—dipped in garlic oil and with crosses etched into them. We all had several smaller knives in sheaths lining our belts. And Peter had this crazy idea to mix vodka and garlic oil together to act as a flammable agent that would both burn—with flames—and corrode the vampire's skin with the garlic, which basically acts like battery acid on them. He put the stuff in those plastic water bottles you see joggers carrying and jerry-rigged some ridiculous harness to carry them on his torso. Lizzy—our resident vampire expert—didn't call him nuts, but she didn't seem overly impressed with the idea either. Maybe she was just old school. Who knows? But that's what we had. That, and my little extra insurance policy I carried in an ankle holster.

I should probably throw in a word or two about crosses. It's an established fact that Dracula is repelled by the cross. But there's a caveat to the cross deal. The person holding the cross has to have some sort of faith. I would guess it's the Christian faith. You know, it being a cross and all. But it's not just a passing Christmas and Easter variety of faith. The person has to truly believe in this power or in God or something like that. None of us really fit the bill. My dad did in his own kind of homegrown way. I'd never known him to attend a church service, but he prayed and read scripture. He wore a cross and had some success against vampires with it. I do know it helped him against Dracula in the past. Probably saved his skin at one point. In fact, I think it might be the reason Dracula ordered Peter to kill my dad instead of doing it himself. He had those crazy crosses painted on his face and it obviously had some impact on the vampire.

But that worked for him. At least until Dracula found a way around it. But not us. Not really. You might think us stupid. I mean, this is something proven to work so why not dive headlong into the faith thing. But real belief doesn't work like that. It can't just be on the intellectual level but must be on the heart level as well. You've got to truly buy into it full on. I guess none of us were ever really able to make that leap. So, needless to say, we had crosses etched on our blades but we didn't carry them around our necks. It just wouldn't work. Kind of cockeyed, really. I don't even know why they were on our blades other than that's what my dad always did.

One of our big concerns was Peter. It had been over a year since the events in Wallachia, we hadn't seen any evidence of Dracula's influence on the guy, but the reality was that my cousin had been Dracula's mind slave. So much so that he'd killed my dad at Dracula's command. We didn't want to walk into this situation only to find that Peter was suddenly under the vampire's thrall and gunning for us with a bloodlust and a death wish.

This alone, in my eyes, was enough to stop the whole venture, but Lizzy and Peter were all hopped up on the idea of rescuing the two girls and staking Dracula once and for all.

Yay them.

Lizzy's solution was to hypnotize Peter. Weirdly enough, she'd encountered this situation before and had learned the art of hypnosis just for times like this.

My mom led a strange life.

The process was actually pretty quick and Lizzy felt confident that should Dracula attempt to influence Peter that my cousin would simply lock the Dracula voice in a little box in some dusty corner of his brain and throw away the key. Nice, I guess. I wasn't buying it, though. Too much chance of a major backfire. I, for one, like to be able to trust the people who are supposed to have my back. Throwing in with the guy that knifed my dad doesn't quite fit that bill.

Dracula's place ended up being a warehouse on the south side. Not a great neighborhood, but we weren't there for a Sunday brunch.

We got there early, maybe one in the afternoon, plenty of daylight left. We had no desire to confront Dracula while he was awake. But this was Dracula we were hunting. The guy hadn't survived for six centuries by being careless. The place was essentially a tomb. Or at least a trap. Lizzy picked the lock easily enough. She was actually pretty impressive. But once inside we knew immediately that we were in trouble. There was no inner handle on the door we'd just come through. It had, of course, locked behind us before we'd realized this, sealing us in. There were no windows to break and escape through, the single garage door had been walled off, and there were no other doors leading to the outside. There we stood in this large nearly empty space. Trapped. Cinderblock walls, florescent lighting. Concrete floor. There were what appeared to be stainless steel coolers at the far end of the room.

And then there was the other stuff. The holy-shit-what-the-hell-have-we-stumbled-into stuff. Chains and shackles lined the western wall. There were two corpses hanging there, one male one female, hands shackled, long gashes in their necks, both nearly naked and striped of large patches of skin. Smelled like week-old meat. A stainless steel table stood near the center of the room. There were leather straps dangling from the sides. The floor was stained red beneath. A human arm lay about four feet to the left. It looked like it'd been gnawed on by a pack of dogs.

"Strange," said Lizzy.

I glared at her. "You expected what? Disneyland?"

"What I mean is, this isn't like Dracula."

"No. You're right," said Peter. "Dracula has always been about his royalty. Prestige, status, the guy's an egomaniac. This is disturbing. There's no class here, nothing designed to impress."

"Oh, he's trying to impress us," said Lizzy. "But not with his stature. He wants us to be impressed with just how ruthless he can be. He wants us terrified."

I said, "So, Vlad the Impaler is worried that we don't know he's a badass?"

Lizzy ignored me and moved past the gore-fest to the coolers. "They're in here," she said.

"Who? Anica and Kerri?" asked Peter.

"If they are," I said. "Then they're already fang heads. You don't keep humans in coolers."

Lizzy said, "The cooling systems could be turned off. They could be used as holding cells. We can't assume anything yet. But, for the record, I was talking about the vampires being in the coolers, not our friends."

I said, "Well, glad you clarified that. Ever consider they might be one and the same?"

Choosing not to reply, Lizzy lowered her backpack to the floor, opening it and withdrawing some tools. A handsaw, screwdrivers, that sort of thing. Immediately, she began working on the cooler door handles. But these handles weren't your common Home Depot variety. These were more of the maximum security kind. There were no screws to unscrew. There was no gap to pry open, no keyhole to pick. The metal was thick and durable. The sawblade broke almost as soon as Lizzy began hacking away at it.

But she kept at it. More than an hour, just trying one thing after another. I felt like a goof standing there handing her each tool she requested like some wannabe surgical nurse in training. I guess that still made me more productive than Peter who basically wandered around the room looking for secret passages. But I was ready to climb up a wall. The place reeked like Hell on a holiday and I had to keep swallowing my rising puke.

But worse was that this was an obvious trap. Lizzy said that she, my dad, and uncles, were in a similar situation back in the seventies. Locked in until the vampires rose, at which point they had to fight for their lives. The fact that they'd only lost one man—my Uncle Chaz—that night didn't comfort me much. Plenty of Van Helsings have died at the hands of vampires. I'd spent my life trying to avoid becoming one of them. And now, well, look where I ended up.

And I wasn't just trying to save my own skin—though that was preferable. The truth of it is, I didn't want to lose Lizzy. She probably never could have won mom of the year. Even after she'd quit hunting vampires she still had her own thing going on. Helping to run the family business and all that. We've never been close. But, yeah, there was always love. Flowing both ways. I don't think either of us were ever that hot at expressing it, but we knew it was there. And now we were about to take on Dracula, and my mom was old, and there's rarely been an encounter with this fiend that didn't end in the death of someone from my family.

Like my dad.

Just a little over a year ago and it still stings like a bitch. I see his face every time I close my eyes. I hear his voice when I speak. Funny, I never realized how many phrases and quirks I stole from him. So yeah, I wasn't on the let's-take-out-Dracula bandwagon. Peter, I could pretty much care less about, but Lizzy, she was the only reason I was there. Just too big of a risk of losing her. I had to throw myself into the mix. Try to keep this thing from going south.

Lizzy eventually gave up on the cooler doors. Peter had scoped out the entire place and found no way out. So glad he was thorough. All that was left for us to do was to wait.

FYI, waiting sucks.

There's nothing to do but to think about what comes next. And in my book that was a battle for our lives against the most notorious vampire in history, the vampire responsible for the deaths of nearly my entire family line. Lizzy, God bless her, tried to give us a pep talk. She talked strategy and made sure we had weapons in hand and game faces on. But let's be real, she was the only pro here—and she was over seventy years-old. Put an old and creaky Michael Jordan with a team of enthusiastic amateurs and pit them against any NBA team in the league and the outcome is a forgone conclusion. Doesn't matter what you did in your glory days, you ain't got a chance today. If we'd been able to get to the vamp during daylight, yeah, that was the plan. Maybe it could have gone our way. But this scenario, well, there was no way we'd all survive.

And so night eventually came.

And Dracula exited one of the coolers along with his two new brides, Anica and Kerri. Yeah, they were vampires, and not brand new ones either. According to Lizzy, the ones fresh in the blood, definitely the first few days, maybe even weeks, weren't too with it yet. They were nearly animals. It took a while for the human memories and traits to resurface. So yeah, Lavinia had lied when she'd said the girls were still alive. Big surprise, huh? She knew we wouldn't come if we knew the girls were already lost. But she wanted us there for her own purposes. She wanted us facing off with Dracula.

We'd known what time it was, knew the vamps would be emerging any minute. We were ready for them, more or less. Lizzy had the crossbow, Peter and I had the three foot long blades coated in garlic oil. We all had knives. We stood before the coolers armed and ready.

But, no big surprise, Dracula had known we were there. So he sent rats in as an advance team. They appeared as if from everywhere, every drain, every grate, every vent. In less than thirty seconds they were on us, scurrying, biting, climbing up our legs. We hacked at them with our knives, we stomped on them, but still they kept coming. My blade fell from my hand as I pulled rats from my chest. One got all the way up to my face and chomped on my right cheek. A hunk of flesh ripped from my face when I pulled the thing away from me.

I was still yanking the last two rodents from my body when I realized that the attack was over. The rats had scattered.

Along with our primary weapons.

The arms were still in the room, but well out of easy reach. The rats had carried the crossbow and swords to beside the walls and now just sat silently in little clusters around the room.

And there stood Dracula and his two fledgling vampires.

We just stood there staring at one another, the three vampires and the three humans. All three of us living ones were bleeding from multiple bite wounds. I had my hand pressed against my face, attempting to slow the bleeding and wondering if a cheek could grow back or if I'd look like some kind of freak for the rest of my life—if there was a rest of my life! And there we were, already wounded, defenseless, just staring at the monsters. I'd never been close to either Kerri or Anica. I'd gotten to know them each. But they were connected to the vampire hunting life and I'd wanted to distance myself from all of that. Still, the sight of them caused my stomach to tumble. God, they looked dead. Just dead. Dracula, maybe because he's been a vampire so long, maybe because he's so strong, maybe just because he's Dracula, can pass pretty well as human. If you look closely—real closely—you can pick out that there's something hinky about the guy, but you've got to be looking for it. Lavinia was pretty much the same. No obvious signs.

Not Anica or Kerri, though. Their skin was as white as gym socks in a puddle of bleach, their faces gaunt, their lips pulled back revealing the fangs. They weren't wild-eyed or animalistic like brand new vampires, their movements were humanlike, but their eyes were hollow golf balls in sunken sockets. Their fingers were short and puffy as if they wanted to be paws but weren't quite able. The fingernails were long and yellow.

When Anica spoke, I was shocked at how normal her voice sounded. "You've come to save us," she said. "There is no need. We are content in our new existence."

"You despised Dracula," said Lizzy. "He's responsible for your father's death."

She smiled a hideous smile all teeth and no soul. "Lavinia was responsible for his death. My husband had nothing to do with it. In fact, he slayed her for that act."

Husband, huh? Wow, that vampire bite really did come with a whole toy box full of indoctrination.

Dracula grinned. "Elizabeth Van Helsing, as you can see, the women you seek are now under my care. They are happy and content and no longer of your concern." Lizzy was about to reply, but Dracula held up his index finger indicating for her to hold that comment. "I know," he said. "You will never accept this. You've spent your life pursuing me, as have your entire clan. And now…" He paused spreading his arms as if to welcome us. "Here you are. You do understand this will end here. You are that bright, at least."

I was about to say something typically smartass, but that was when Peter decided to take the offensive and throw a knife at Dracula's chest.

Well, in the general direction of Dracula. His aim wasn't what I would call spot on.

And so all hell broke loose.

The two vampire brides moved immediately to defend their beloved master. Not sure why it went down this way, but they went for Lizzy and me, not Peter—the guy who'd thrown the knife.

Anica was on me before I could say, "Holy shit!" But I was able to get a hand on one of my sheathed blades and swiped left to right across her chest. She let out a howl. I don't know if it was the crosses etched into the metal or the coating of garlic oil, but her skin bubbled and sizzled. I was down with that.

This didn't make her happy and so she chomped down on my left bicep. So I jabbed the same knife into her back. She jerked away, twirling around, reaching for the protruding blade but unable to get a grip on it.

I turned to see Kerri locking her fangs onto Lizzy's neck, blood spattered across her face. I screamed, "Mom!" And nearly leaped toward Kerri, but felt a strong hand grip me at the shoulder and toss me a good ten feet in the opposite direction. Dracula, of course. Amazing, the guy's strength.

I scrambled to my feet, still hoping to get to Lizzy before it was too late. But, Peter was already on it. Somehow he'd made his way to the crossbow. It was in his hands, he aimed, fired.

This time his aim didn't suck. Bam! The bolt hit Kerri mid chest. Her eyes went golf ball-sized for about half a second before she toppled backward, blood oozing from around the bolt, her flesh sizzling from the garlic.

Peter pulled another bolt free and was loading, but Anica, blade still sticking out of her back, nearly flew at him, crashing into him and slamming him to the floor. The crossbow went skittering away and I could see Peter trying to pull one of his knives free of its sheath.

I was moving to help Peter when Lizzy shouted, "Dane! Look out!"

The warning was too late. Dracula was already on me, his teeth penetrating my neck. It was the most surreal feeling. Painful, yeah, but kind of peaceful too. I think it was Dracula's mind mojo. He calmed his victims, nearly—or completely—hypnotizing them. I tried to fight him off, but then, I really didn't try too hard. I was just sort of floating in this milky haze.

And then he jerked away from me and the spell was broken. There was Lizzy. She'd pulled her Bowie knife out and jabbed it into Dracula's back. But she'd missed the heart. The thing was sticking out just below the shoulder. A similar strike to what I'd inflicted on Kerri. She was already drawing another blade, preparing to finish him off, but then…

Well, here's where it gets real.

It was the most horrific thing I'd ever seen in my life and it was done to my mother.

And there wasn't a damn thing I could do about it.

I'd known that Dracula could shapeshift. Everyone's heard of him turning into a bat or a wolf, or even just melting away into a mist. But I'd never heard of anything like this.

He shimmered, just glittering for a couple of seconds. And then it seemed as if he was falling apart, or maybe disintegrating is a better word. It was like the glue holding all of his particles together just came undone. Like someone took a dustpan full of dust and tossed it into the air. The knife that had been in Dracula's back clattered to the floor as these little insect-sized particles twirled and dove.

It took me a moment to realize what had just happened. Mosquitoes. Dracula had transformed into a swarm of mosquitoes. It was like a cloud of insects. And they descended on Lizzy.

She screamed. Oh, God, did she scream. She was being bitten on every inch of her body. The gray cloud of mosquitoes became red as they sucked the blood from her body. I raced to her, attempting to pull her free, but the swarm stayed with her. I can't say why I wasn't bitten. Maybe Dracula could only focus on one victim at a time while in this form. Maybe, even though he'd become hundreds of tiny beings, he was still, in essence, one entity and therefore constrained by the confines of a single body despite his current state.

Regardless, there was nothing I could do. I slashed at the things with my knife, but what good is a knife against a swarm of insects? I'd waded into the middle of it and was soon covered with my mother's blood. God, there was so much blood. It was as if it was just floating there, amidst the mosquitoes yet separate, like they weren't really ingesting it, but just freeing it from her body, creating a cloud of red haze. Her screams were soon whimpers and I dropped to the floor beside her as she gasped her last. I don't even know if she was aware that I was there. Her eyes were open, but glassy, probably sightless. Her mouth opened and closed like she was a fish on the deck of a boat. No sound, no words, just open, shut, open, shut. I squeezed her hand, but she didn't squeeze back. Her hand was limp, already getting cold for lack of blood. I screamed and slashed away at the mosquitoes with my useless knife, but neither the blade nor my tears could change what had happened. My mom was dead. I hadn't even fully processed my dad's death of a year earlier and here was Mom. Cold and lifeless and gone. Forever gone.

I was only half aware of my surroundings as the cloud of insects swirled away and began to reform into Dracula. At the time I didn't think about it, why he didn't simply maintain that seemingly invincible form. Maybe it was too much of a strain on him, maybe he could only maintain that state for a short time, but I wasn't thinking of any of that just then.

My focus was on Mom.

At least until Peter disrupted the moment in spectacular fashion.

My cousin had managed to slosh his vodka-garlic cocktail over Anica and was jabbing a Bic lighter in the vampire's direction. She went up like a torch, her entire frame bursting into flames. She screamed and twirled around batting at her own personal blaze. Then she collided with the metal table at the center of the room, crashing to the floor beside it.

Dracula howled as if it was he himself that had been set ablaze. "Anica!" he cried. "My Anica!" I felt no sympathy for the bastard as he raced toward his blazing bride and fell to his knees beside her dying form. I was still cradling my dead mother. Dracula's misery was no concern to me. In truth, in that moment, I couldn't even take joy in his suffering. I was numb, my mind in a fog. I should have relished in his misery, but right then, he was a nonentity.

Peter was withdrawing another of his water bottle firebombs when Dracula rose, thrusting the thing away from him and clasping Peter's neck. "Gut yourself," said Dracula. "Take one of your blades and disembowel yourself.

Peter's eyes fluttered. I assume he was attempting to fight Dracula's influence. It was clutch time and I had no idea if Lizzy's hypnotism would hold.

"I said open your gullet," sneered the vampire.

Peter's jaw went slack. His right arm jittered and jerked, but his hand was moving toward the sheathed blades. Damn it, he was giving in.

Dracula grinned. "Good, good. Take the blade in hand. Slice yourself open." As angry as he'd been, it appeared that Dracula had already forgotten his still flaming bride who was only ten feet distant.

Peter's arm lifted. He held the blade. It was positioned toward his own gut.

And then my cousin said, "No," and allowed the knife to fall to the floor. I don't know why he didn't just jab Dracula. Maybe he was only able to gain enough control to release the blade, but not enough to attack that disgusting freak of nature.

"You slew her!" screamed Dracula as he lifted Peter from the ground with only the hand clasped at my cousin's throat. "My love! You killed my love."

Neither of them noticed the vampiric mist descending from a ceiling vent and taking form behind Dracula. He would have killed Peter then, I'm sure of it. He either would have simply snapped his neck with a single squeeze or slashed his throat with his fangs. The only reason Peter didn't die in that instant was Lavinia.

"Oh please," said the now fully-formed vampire. "No one has ever been your love, only your obsession."

Dropping Peter, Dracula whirled to face her. "Lavinia!" His expression betrayed his shock.

"Here to serve you, my Lord." The tone was condescending, the exaggerated bow patronizing.

To Dracula's credit, he regained his composure almost immediately. "I am surprised to see you here," he said.

Lavinia nodded. "You can say it, Vlad. You thought me dead. You preferred me dead. You had a new plaything and you thought you had finally found that ever elusive love." She shook her head like a mother instructing a naughty child. "But if there is such a thing as love among our kind, then it is the thing we once shared, you and I. Oh, I will never claim it to be pure or truly meaningful. I see it as more of a mutual lust, both for each other and for the blood we took together. Human love, whatever that is—if it even truly exists—is forever lost to us. But you have always been the fool when it comes to these things. You see a pretty young thing and mistake desire for affection. You may be the greatest most celebrated among our kind, but you have always been a child at best. Tantrums and demands. Me, Anica, any of us, we were nothing but new toys to you, nothing more. And now you will have to settle for an old and worn plaything, but one that simply will not go away."

Dracula's expression was one of bemused interest. I'm sure he bristled at the insults and I doubt anyone else could have gotten away with it. And so he just gazed at her. No words, just the hint of a curious grin on his lips.

Lavinia stepped forward, a saucy grin on her own lips. "So, Vlad. Will you take your throwaway back or did I come all this way in error?"

She came to him, tickled his chin with her left index finger. But there was something that I'd noticed that Dracula had not yet caught. Lavinia's right hand. That tricky bitch had a claw, I mean a full on claw—like from a lion or a tiger—in place of her right hand. Instead of transforming fully into a jungle cat, she'd somehow contained it to the single hand. Despite myself, I actually grinned as Lavinia said, "Don't worry about answering, Vlad. Because I would never have you again. This is not a reunion, you spoiled child. This is revenge."

And the clawed hand raked Dracula's chest, left, right, left, right, shredding him, digging deep into his organs, surely his heart was rent. The vampire had been completely fooled. Even as he sought to push her away, she dug further and further in, twisting, pulling, gauging. Blood pulsed from the multiple wounds, bathing them both. Dracula squirmed as she twisted her arm in three quick jerks and then pulled something from his chest. Not the heart. Maybe his liver. I couldn't really tell. Dracula stared in disbelief as Lavinia brought the oozing mass of meat to her face and took a chomp out of it. Blood and gore spat across her smiling face as she chewed.

I'd seen plenty. My shock had worn off. And I sure didn't want to see what Lavinia had in mind for us. Dracula was somehow still standing. He was actually stepping forward, reaching for Lavinia. "You always saw yourself as something more than…" But he couldn't finish the sentence. His legs faltered. His skin was pulling tighter across his face, beginning to disintegrate. Obviously she'd ruined his heart, that one all-important organ necessary for his survival. Lavinia was laughing at him, still gnawing on the meat when I pulled the little pistol from my ankle holster and put five shells through her chest. She jerked left and then right as the bullets struck. The organ dropped from her hand. She turned toward me, took a step, but faltered, barely maintaining her balance.

Lizzy had always warned against using guns against vampires. Her mom (my grandmother) had accidently shot her husband when Dracula had dematerialized just as she'd fired a shot. The bullet had sailed through the vampire's immaterial form and struck my grandfather. The wound hadn't been fatal, but it had resulted in the no guns policy.

I wasn't big on policy.

They both, Dracula and Lavinia, were centuries old and so deteriorated into a fine gray powder. It took a couple of minutes for the whole process, sure. But they were to the floor within seconds. Both eyeing the other accusingly, Dracula grabbing at his deteriorating organ and trying to cram it back into his skeletal chest. But his ribs cracked and then crumbled at the pressure. And then the organ was little more than mucus, and then dust. Dracula reached toward me, pulling himself forward in a disjointed crawl. The lower half of his body had already detached, but still he tried to reach me, his jaw snapping, the teeth breaking and crumbling, and then there was nothing left of him but scattered dirt.

Peter was already in motion by the time I'd made my way to the two piles of vamp dust. He bent, pulling and tugging at Dracula's clothing as if in search of something before pouring his fire juice over the ashes and pulling another bottle from his harness. "Here," he said, handing me one of the plastic bottles. "We need to separate heads from bodies and burn all of the vampire carcasses." He hesitated and then added. "That probably means your mom too. I'm not sure if she'd be infected or not. The mosquitoes, I've never heard of that phenomenon before."

I won't go into details. You wouldn't much like the language and the descriptions of what we were forced to do. This was stuff to make a B movie buff's stomach turn. But, we did the deed. All of it. Mom included. God, I don't know if I'll ever be able to look myself in the mirror again. I just don't know.

Random notes from Peter Van Helsing written on scraps of paper, furniture surfaces, and the walls of his apartment July 12-August 06, 2015

There are things that nobody knows about that last night. Yeah, the night my aunt Lizzy Mulligan died. And, more importantly to some people, but not to me, that Dracula died. Oh, don't get the impression that Dracula's death is insignificant. No. It was crucial. I guess you could call it historic. Who can know how many hundreds—maybe even thousands—of people have died as a result of that monster? Oh, it wouldn't be overstating my case to say that his death was as necessary as Hitler's or Bin Laden's.

But Lizzy's death was personal. I'd come to love her over these past several months. And it was on that horrific night that I finally got to see her for who she truly was. Not the grieving widow. Not the broken lifeless soul of the past year. But the fighter. The leader, the woman who would willingly face the devil himself. And who but Dracula is more like Satan? Old Scratch, the prince of evil. Lord of Flies. She, Lizzy I mean, was old, but there was still so much more life in her. All of this is probably even more significant in light of the fact that my children, most definitely spurred on by my ex-wife—who is certainly next in line for that Satan designation - have stopped all communication with me. There's an injunction against me preventing me from seeing them. Even my own mother, after learning that I'd come back from my adventure relatively intact, has all but abandoned me. I'm a disappointment, she says. It's my fault that she estranged from her grandchildren. And so, the aunt I'd never known became my family.

But this isn't about Lizzy, my kids, or even about my wacked out feelings about any of this. Nah, this is about Dracula's "death."

Yeah, I put quotation marks around the word death. I'll get to that. But first, here are some details no one knows about that night.

Stop. Maybe I should explain my state of mind.

While in Europe, I'd been Dracula's mind thrall. Horrible, just awful. Insane! Lizzy's take was that the spell had been broken by time and distance. But I always feared that if I got close to him again that he'd regain control. Lizzy hypnotized me to prevent this. And it worked as well as could be expected.

But Dracula was fighting for control from the moment we neared his lair. I bet he even viewed our progress through my eyes. No. I mean, I can't be sure, but the possibility was there. Probable even. I was totally freaked when we got into that place. And even more so when I felt him nettling around in my brain. Just, poke, poke, poke. An idea here, a suggestion there. God, I nearly went nuts. There was even a point where I almost turned my blade on Lizzy as well as on myself.

But I fought him. And God, I'm not trying to sound conceited, but I managed to beat the creep. Kind of. But maybe not entirely.

Well, Okay. Lay the cards on the table, Peter. Here's the thing I've been dancing around. After Dracula was dead. When he was just dust, I felt this crazy need to rescue his journal. Oh, I told myself that it was so that we could have it translated and added to the collection of documents which contained earlier journal entries by the vampire. And I did this. I hired a Romanian linguist to translate the portions of the journal that weren't in English. Dracula tended to float between his known languages when he wrote. I think he'd spent so much time in America that English had almost become a native tongue to him. So, bits in English, bits in Romanian or some earlier form of the language. I was never quite sure what was what.

I told myself that I would destroy the original journal after the translation was complete. This was important because the journal itself, centuries ago, had been, what would be the right word? Enchanted. Hexed? Bewitched? God, I don't know. But the result was that through the spilling of Dracula's own blood on the pages and some crazy mystical enchantments, the journal was able to carry the essence of Dracula's soul. This meant it could be used to resurrect the vampire. Yeah. It's been used this way in the past—most notably by my great uncle Charlie. I'm not anxious for it to happen again.

But the translation's been completed for over a week now. And I haven't destroyed the book. Oh, I've tried several times. Of course I have. I've set the fireplace ablaze, brought the book to within inches of the flames, but it's never gone further than that. I tell myself that I'm hesitant to destroy such an important historical document. This is the actual journal of Vlad Dracula. The Impaler. The vampire. Its existence might actually prove to the world that the vampire truly existed. It could be one of the most important historical documents of all time.

But it could also potentially bring him back.

Oh! Here's an important tidbit. I have his ashes. Yeah. Ashes. You see. Like my ancestor, Abraham Van Helsing, I found that Dracula's ashes are protected from scattering. It's as if they're held together by some insane magnetism. I swept them into two piles and they immediately scooted back together. Very creepy. I put them in separate containers and the containers eroded—within days—and the ashes found their partners.

It was nuts.

What else could I do? I guess I could try taking some of them out onto Lake Michigan. Massive body of water. And then, maybe I could fly another portion to, oh, let's say Peru. Why not? Peru's as good as anyplace, right? Lots of sun there.

But, why didn't I?

Because I'm weak. Boom! There. I said it. Dracula's dead as dirt and yet he still has enough hold on me to prevent me from doing something that would eliminate him permanently.

So, all this to say that the journal's the key. The ashes are the base elements of Dracula's body, but the journal holds the power to reinfuse it with his soul. And I possess both of these elements.

And so I've decided that I'll do it today. Destroy the journal. Right at the peak of the day when the sun is its strongest. Because it's then that I feel the creeping gnaw of Dracula's evil the least. Crazy, isn't it, that even in death he's stronger in the nighttime hours.

***

I did it. I destroyed the journal. The sucker's gone. Finally gone.

***

Alright. Here it is. I'm not being entirely truthful. Well, at least not in the last little blurb I wrote. The one up there by the air vent. I did destroy the journal. Oh, absolutely. Well, most of it. All but one page. Just a single page. Nothing more. There can't be anything wrong with that, can there? A single page. Containing Dracula's dried blood.

***

I'm scared. I'm crazy scared. Maybe more frightened than I was even when held captive as Dracula's thrall.

It's the blood. That damn blood. I've done something stupid. Entirely idiotic. I've read all of the compiled journals and documents. Everything the Van Helsings have collected for all of these decades.

I knew the danger. Oh, yeah. Of course I knew the danger. Even an idiot could figure this out.

I've read of how my great uncle Charlie was enticed to scrape the blood from the journal page, to take that crusty matter that once flowed through the vampire's veins and touch it to his tongue. I've read of how the madness followed, of how he became a slave to the dead vampire and of how he was eventually led to resurrect this sleeping demon.

I knew all of this.

And still I tasted the blood. That same blood. That same crusty demon stuff. I scraped it right off the page and put it on my tongue.

My God, what am I going to do now? What can I possibly do?

***

I can't sleep. Not at night, at least. Maybe small snatches during the daylight hours. I'm not really sure. Everything's fuzzy. You know fuzzy, right? Like those dice people used to hang from their rearview mirrors. Fuzzy! Fuzzy! That's such a fun word. Fuzzy!

***

I think I must be eating more of the blood. The vampire blood. I don't remember doing it. At least, I don't think I remember doing it. I'm not really sure what I remember anymore. But there's less of the blood on the page. In fact, a full corner of the page—a spot that contained the largest concentration of the dried blood—has been gnawed away. Like a dog. A puppy! You know how puppies chew everything. Just gnaw, gnaw, gnaw. It's like a puppy chewed the corner of the page away.

I'm pretty sure I'm the puppy.

Bad dog!

***

I can't stand the sunlight any longer. No, no. No sun. Just, no. It burns. It just burns. How did I ever enjoy it? The sun is so foul. It's disgusting. Bright and flame-like. How could anyone enjoy such a thing?

***

Flies. Flies, flies, flies. Tasty little flies. Tasty, tasty, flies, flies. Tasty yum-yum.

***

I'm sick. Truly sick. Vomiting everywhere. But then why do I feel so invigorated? So alive! So energized! I think I like it. I do, I do. I think I like it.

***

Dear, Steve and Pricilla,

This is for you, my dear dear children. This right here, this note that I am writing right now. Steve, Pricilla, the only two people that matter in all of the world. Pricilla. Such a silly name. It sounds like prissy. Prissy Pricilla. Your mother named you. We didn't agree but she won the argument. She always won the arguments.

I'm sorry. That was probably wrong of me to put that in writing. I'm not, well, I suppose you could say I'm not well. Maybe we could say I have a blood disease. Yes. That's what we'll call it, a blood disease. That sounds so much better than thrall to a dead demon, doesn't it?

Kids, I know you probably hate me. Or, well, at the very least, you don't understand me, or are hurt by me. Disgusted by me? I hope not. I understand. Of course, I understand. You really don't know much about anything that's happened.

I won't take this time to try to turn you away from your lying, Satan, witch, bitch, evil, spiteful damn-her-to-hell mother. Though, I'm sure she's done everything she can to turn you away from me.

Oh, the lies she's probably told you. And they are lies. Oh, trust me. Lies, lies, lies.

But, what I'm trying to say here is that everything I did was done for you. Yes. Even the vampire hunting. Maybe especially that. You see, I wanted you to be proud of me. I wanted you to see me as someone capable of great deeds. Not as a man who drifts from job to job and can't even keep a wife. I wanted you to be proud of me. And to love me. That's all that has ever mattered, is that the two of you love and respect me.

But, I've screwed everything up. All of it. And through it all, you've lost what little respect you might have had for me.

No. Don't feel guilty. Not one iota of guilt. None. I know this was my fault. All my fault. I didn't communicate what I was feeling to you. I didn't share with you my dreams for your lives, or of how proud I am of you both. I didn't tell you of the surge of happiness that overcomes me every time I see you. Or of how just hearing your voices on old voicemail recordings—I've saved them all—brings a smile to my face. I didn't tell you how deeply I love you. And that was wrong of me. Criminal even. All I can say is that you two are my everything. And that I love you more than life itself.

And, Pricilla. I'm sorry, you know, about what I said about your name. I probably would have picked something completely hideous like Gertrude. Or Dorcas! You're perfect as you are. Perfect Pricilla.

I love you both.

Dad

***

I think I've lost about four days. I'm not sure what happened during any of that time but apparently I went about collecting items which, I assume, are to be used in Dracula's resurrection.

The room is filled with strange oils and herbs. There's an ancient book written in a foreign language. Old! Dusty. Threadbare. Gray, with bizarre symbols hand drawn across both front and back. And I wonder, how is it that it came into my possession? Where could I have found it? Did Dracula have it stashed away somewhere? Did I find it on EBay? I'm certain it must contain some sort of incantation.

I don't know what to do. I've obviously lost myself completely. Completely! I fear I'm on the eve of resurrecting this beast and I don't know that I have the self-control to stop myself.

***

I've come to a decision. It's not a happy decision, quite the opposite. But necessary. I am Dracula's human instrument. To my knowledge there are currently no others. Therefore, even with all of the herbs and concoctions he's directed me to assemble, nothing can be done without me being here to bring it all together.

Therefore, I must subtract myself from the equation.

So, this is farewell. I'm not suicidal. I would prefer to live a long and productive life. But, contrary to every impulse in my body and mind, my intent is to take my life as soon as I put this pen down. I've thrown the ancient book into the fireplace and am even now watching it burn—and resisting the near overwhelming impulse to reach in there and pull it out.

But destroying the book is a temporary solution. I know there must be another. Perhaps not the same volume, but one that would serve the same purpose, contain the same mystic information. Maybe not a single volume, maybe a dozen, but I know that I'd find a way to reconstruct the needed resurrection incantation.

And so I must eliminate the only living person who has ingested Dracula's blood. It's the only way.

Pricilla, Steve, I'm so sorry. I wish I had been stronger for you.

Dane, if there's anything left of Dracula out there, you must destroy it. Please. Do not let this continue.

I'm sorry. For all of it. For all of the people we've lost due to my foolishness. I'm so very sorry.

***

I'm still here. Alive. So far, at least. I couldn't do it. Couldn't "subtract myself from the equation." Maybe I'm too cowardly. Maybe just pure survival instinct is keeping me from taking my life. Though, whose survival instinct is in play, mine or Dracula's, could be the subject of a hot debate.

***

As you may have guessed, I didn't destroy the book. Not all of it. As with Dracula's journal, I held back a page. A single page. The rest of the book, into the fire. Such a blaze. It sparked green and blue. It fizzed and sputtered before finally gasping a final breath. But this one page. This one damn page. The needed spell I presume. What else would it be?

In another language.

I can't read it. And yet I do. I stare at it. For hours. Just sitting there staring. Staring. I don't know why. But then I do know, don't I? I'm sure I do. It's my ruin. I don't know what form it will take. But this page is the end of me. I'm certain of it.

And yet I cling to it as if it holds my very salvation.

While it pulls me closer and closer to my damnation.

***

Something is happening to me. I'm not sure what. But I'm frightened. Very frightened. It's almost as if my body is decaying. Like I'm dead. Just dead flesh. It's rank. And I have very little sensation. I even pulled small bits of flesh away from my arm. No sensation. I wanted to call an ambulance, but I couldn't bring myself to pick up the phone. It was as if it was forbidden to me. As if the phone would seize me, electrocute me or bludgeon me. I couldn't bring myself to hold it.

I don't know how much longer I'll be able to continue with these notes. Every word is an agony now. My handwriting is barely legible. My arm is a great weight, my flesh corrupting, decaying, changing. To what I don't know. But the effort is becoming too great.

I feel I am truly lost. A lost soul. No hope for redemption. Just lost. And gone.

This single journal entry was found on September 18, 2015 by a private investigator hired by Steve Kubler. It was located in a New York apartment leased to Mr. Kubler's missing father, Peter Van Helsing. The investigator had been hired by Mr. Kubler to locate his father. Though a photograph of this entry was emailed to Mr. Kubler, the investigator has not been seen or heard from since.

THE JOURNAL ENTRY:

My name is Peter Van Helsing. Or, at least, that is who people will assume me to be. I am in a new city where no one knows me and so there will be no expectations based on already established behavior patterns. And so who would note that I am only seen at night? Who would notice that my eyes now have a tint, ever so slightly, of red, or that I carry myself with a confidence never known to the former Peter Van Helsing?

This body is not ideal. Not near as sturdy as my original form. But Peter was not unhealthy and his age not advanced. As far as the world is concerned, Dracula is dead. This is best. Celebrity has no draw. And in this present age, there is little need for title or pomp. My monetary needs can be acquired through mind thralls as can any other necessities. I am meant to live amidst the shadows, to steal about the night. To live as I please with little regard for the hordes of humanity about me. And so it is best that I am anonymous as I continue forward in this dark and beautiful eternal midnight.

Coming in 2020!

By Thom Reese

THE VOYAGE OF THE AMETHYST CASTLE

A mystical world filled with magic and
mystery in a castle floating on the sea!

At once, whimsical, quirky, and action-packed, *The Voyage of the Amethyst Castle* is a manic romp through a unique and enchanted world that is guaranteed to capture the imaginations of all.

FIRES OF THE ATESI
A Huntington Novel

Marc and Dana Huntington are back in an adventure
that is perhaps the most significant in their careers!

An ancient relic imbued with miraculous power!

A mysterious adversary with abilities approaching the astounding!

All of Earth held in the balance!

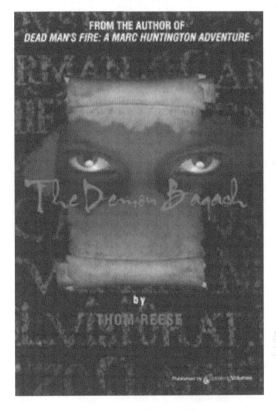

On Sale Now!

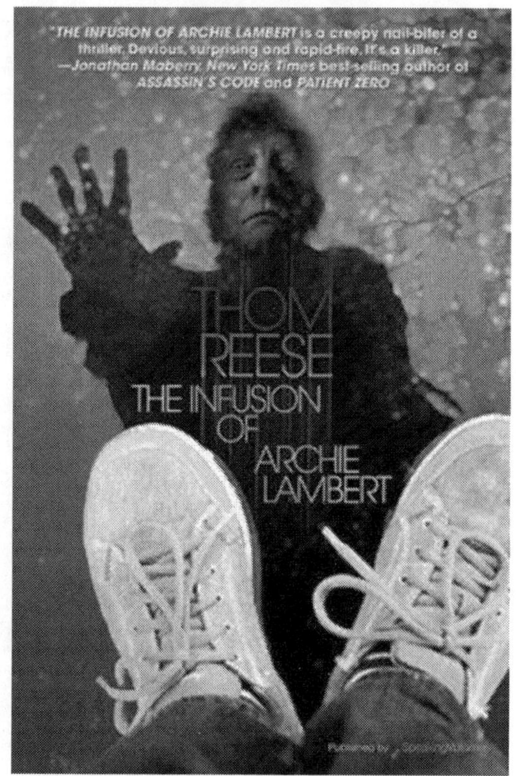

For more information
visit: www.SpeakingVolumes.us

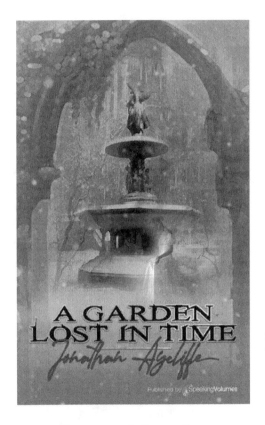

Made in the USA
Las Vegas, NV
28 November 2023

81698927R00090